RECOMMENDED for You

RECOMMENDED
for You

Laura Silverman

Margaret K. McElderry Books
New York   London   Toronto   Sydney   New Delhi

MARGARET K. McELDERRY BOOKS

An imprint of Simon & Schuster Children's Publishing Division

1230 Avenue of the Americas, New York, New York 10020

MARGARET K. McELDERRY BOOKS is a trademark of Simon & Schuster, Inc.

For information about special discounts for bulk purchases, please contact Simon & Schuster Special Sales at 1-866-506-1949 or business@simonandschuster.com.

The Simon & Schuster Speakers Bureau can bring authors to your live event. For more information or to book an event, contact the Simon & Schuster Speakers Bureau at 1-866-248-3049 or visit our website at www.simonspeakers.com.

Book design by Debra Sfetsios-Conover

The text for this book was set in Adobe Garamond Pro.

Manufactured in the United States of America

First Edition

10 9 8 7 6 5 4 3 2 1

Library of Congress Cataloging-in-Publication Data

Names: Silverman, Laura, author.

Title: Recommended for you / Laura Silverman.

Description: First edition. | New York : Margaret K. McElderry Books, [2020] | Audience: Ages 12 up. | Audience: Grades 7–9. | Summary: Shoshanna Greenburg loves her job at the bookstore, Once Upon, until Jake Kaplan joins the staff, a handsome nonreader who challenges her for a bonus she needs.

Identifiers: LCCN 2020004048 (print) | ISBN 9781534474192 (hardcover) | ISBN 9781534474215 (eBook)

Subjects: CYAC: Bookstores—Fiction. | Competition (Psychology)—Fiction. | Jews—United States—Fiction. | Lesbian mothers—Fiction.

Classification: LCC PZ7.1.S543 Rec 2020 (print) | DDC [Fic]—dc23

LC record available at https://lccn.loc.gov/2020004048

For Phillip—

Thank you for always encouraging my love of writing.
You were the best brother in the world, and we didn't get enough
time together. I'll love and miss you forever.

Your sister,
Laura

Chapter One

Barbra Streisand grinds and grinds before sputtering to a stop.

"Ugh!" I call out, and then plead with my car. "Barbra, sweetie." I place my hand on her dashboard and rub in soothing circles. "I need you to start. I'm going to be late for work. Will you start for me? Pretty please? Okay, ready?"

I turn the keys again. The grinding sound is worse this time, metallic shrieking. "Darn you!" I yank out the key. It's a freezing December morning, and as I exhale, I can see my frosted breath.

My phone buzzes with a text from Cheyenne: I just folded my 75th sweater of the morning. When do you get here?

The mall opens earlier than usual this week for the Christmas rush. Cheyenne has already been folding clothes at the Gap for an hour, and I'm supposed to be at Once Upon, the independent bookstore I work at, in twenty minutes.

I text back: Hopefully soon! Barbra won't start

She replies: Rough! I'll drive you home later

I send her an emoji kiss face, then step out of my car, tug my coat tight, and hurry inside. Mom and Mama are still home, but the house is silent. I peek into the living room first, then the kitchen. Nothing. I thud upstairs to their bedroom, but the door is shut. Muffled voices filter into the hallway at an inaudible murmur. Usually their door is open. Usually I'd waltz right inside and jump on their bed, playing with the tassels of a throw pillow while asking for a ride. But now their door is closed, dampening the tense voices inside.

I take a short breath, then square my shoulders and knock with two quick raps.

The voices stop, and moments later, Mom opens the door. We have the same brown eyes and the same curly brown hair, but her eyes are tired, and her hair is pulled back into a frizzy braid. It really needs a deep condition. I want to recommend a recipe for a great avocado hair mask I found online, but reading the room, now is not the time for hair-care essentials.

"Shoshanna," Mom says. "Aren't you supposed to be at work?"

Her voice almost snaps, like she's mad at me or something. I fiddle with my Star of David necklace and rock back on my heels. "Barbra won't start. Again. Can I get a ride to the mall?"

"That car should've been junked years ago," Mom mutters.

My pulse skips. She can't junk Barbra Streisand. Yes, she's

old, passed down from my moms to me, but I need a car, and my Once Upon paycheck doesn't cover much more than gas and insurance. "Um." I clear my throat. "I don't want to be late. Christmas rush and all."

Mama walks over to us. Her blond hair is still wet from the shower, and she's wearing her silk peach bathrobe, cinched lightly above her rounded hips. It's strange, both of them standing by the cracked door, bare feet on their bedroom carpet, while I'm here in the hallway, boots on the hardwood floor.

"I wish I could take you," Mama says. "But I'm teaching a class soon and need to get ready. Sorry, love."

I give her a small smile. "That's okay, Mama."

"Fine." Mom's voice does snap this time. "I'll take you on the way to work, then. I'll be downstairs in five."

"Okay." I twist my fingers together. "Thanks."

Mom nods and slides back into the room, closing the door behind her. Their murmurs continue, slightly louder than before. I catch a snippet about dirty dishes. Dishes? Is that really why they're arguing?

I walk downstairs, but instead of going straight to the garage, I head into the kitchen. The coffeepot sits in the sink. Next to it are a spoon and a mug with an ounce of milky coffee at the bottom. It's a silly thing to fight about; I can fix it, just like that, and everyone will be happy. I slip off my coat, pull on our pair of ladybug-patterned dish gloves, and wash and dry each piece.

* * *

Mom pulls to a stop in front of the mall and then slips a lipstick out of her purse. She applies the creamy pink color in two easy strokes. When I was younger, I'd sprawl out on her bedroom floor, rummaging through her countless bags of cosmetics and perfumes, while she sat at her vanity rubbing in moisturizer and lining her eyes with soft brown pencil. It was calm, our little sanctuary.

"Do you need a ride home later?" Mom asks, capping the lipstick. She sees me eyeing it. "Go on."

Tension eases from my shoulders as I take her offering. She's not mad at me. Of course not. It's not like she was going to jump for joy upon hearing Barbra broke down yet again. "Cheyenne can drive me home," I say. "Thanks, though!"

I pull down the passenger mirror and apply the color, immediately smudging some onto my skin. I rub my finger at the corner of my mouth to fix it and try not to feel like a little kid playing dress-up. Then I press my lips together and smile. The color is a much softer pink than my jacket and looks nice with my rosy winter cheeks.

"Pretty," Mom replies. And then, "I need to get to work."

"Right." I place the lipstick in the center console. "Well, thanks for the ride."

I unbuckle my seat belt, grab my tote bag, and slide out of the car. But as I'm about to shut the door, Mom turns to me, her eyes softened. "I'll ask Eve to swing by later, see what it'll take to fix Barbra. Okay?"

I beam. "Okay!" Eve is our family friend and a mechanic. Mom met her in their kickboxing class like a decade ago, and Eve always makes house calls when one of the cars, usually Barbra—okay, always Barbra—needs fixing. "See you at Latkepalooza tonight?"

"Of course," Mom says. "See you tonight."

I shut the door, and Mom gives a quick wave before driving away.

Latkepalooza is our last-night-of-Hanukkah family tradition. We aren't the light-the-candles-all-eight-nights type of Jews, but we make sure to celebrate at least one evening with latkes and dreidel. My moms and I love spending time with each other, whether it's for Latkepalooza, a *90 Day Fiancé* marathon, or a night out bowling. We just click, fitting seamlessly together like the two-thousand-piece puzzle we tackled last year. One summer we even made it through a sixteen-hour road trip to New York without getting into a single argument, which is probably like a world record for traveling families everywhere.

But things have been different lately. Open doors and TLC binges have been replaced with shut doors and arguments. And more common than fighting, there's been silence, all of us disconnected. As Mom drives away, I try to shake off my unease. It's probably nothing. Just petty squabbles over dishes. We've all been busy—Mom works a million hours a week, Mama paints on the screened-in porch, space heater running full blast, often well past dinnertime, and now that it's winter break, even I'm pulling double shifts. But tonight we'll all light the candles and open presents and eat stacks of fried potatoes with applesauce, the best topping, and everything will be good again.

The frigid December air cuts through my jacket as I walk toward the mall entrance. It's barely eight in the morning, but the parking lot is already half full. A silver sedan roams the packed front rows, looking for a close spot. I enter through the east-wing doors and sigh in relief at the burst of warm air. Most of the food court restaurants are still closed, but employees prep in the back, shouting to each other and blasting music. Starbucks is open, the line already fifteen people deep. I'm running late, so I ignore my taste buds begging for a peppermint mocha.

I reach the Gap and spot Cheyenne through the window. Her dark brown skin pops against the display of cream and peach sweaters. She startles when I knock on the glass, then sees me and grins, waving me into the store. I shake my head, saying, "Late! See you at lunch, beautiful!" She blows me a kiss through the window, and I catch it with a smile. We met in the cafeteria in seventh grade when we both went to grab the last slice of cheese pizza. Total rom-com meet-cute moment. We split the slice and talked for all of lunch, topics ranging from our love of *Bob's Burgers* to speculating if there's intelligent life on other planets to confiding in each other about our current crushes, and now our friendship is forever cemented by cheesy goodness.

I keep walking and pass the Disney Store and Pet Depot and H&M and the stand that sells Dead Sea lotions and always has these really hot Israelis working at it, and then finally, I'm here.

Once Upon.

The store marquee is written in blue cursive script, and there are vibrant displays in each window with new releases and old favorites. One of the books is angled a bit too far to the left, making the title hard to read. I make a mental note to fix it as I step into the store. The scent of books and the quiet hum of morning customers browsing the shelves welcome me. My body lifts with contentment. I'm home.

A few hours later, the store is packed with holiday shoppers, and I'm running around nonstop, restocking displays, ringing up customers, and reshelving books in the correct spots because god forbid someone puts a book back where they found it, or at least on a display table, instead of shoving it into a spot on the wrong shelf. On my way to the stockroom, I notice a middle-aged white guy standing in the philosophy section. He's wearing a gray sweater and jeans—and he's taking pictures of a book, one page at a time.

"Excuse me, sir—" I stop short. "You can't do that."

He doesn't even look at me, just flips the page and angles his phone.

"Sir?" I repeat, making sure he hears me.

He glances up this time, but his eyes don't register me as a threat. I guess my five-foot stature and chipmunk-print dress aren't very menacing.

"I'm almost done," he says, taking another picture.

"But you're not allowed to do that." I take a small step forward. "This is a bookstore. A writer worked hard on that book. You can't steal their work without paying for it."

"And yet," he responds, turning another page, "I can."

"Sir, please either take the book to the register or put it back on the shelf."

"*Sweetheart*," he snaps, voice hard and laced with condescension. "Stop talking."

The word "sweetheart" burrows under my skin and makes it burn. Ugh. There's a walkie-talkie attached to my dress pocket, and I want to use it to call security on this guy over the PA system. But this guy is a stranger, and very tall, and the domineering tone of his voice makes me think engaging him further is not a smart idea.

So instead of publicly shaming him, I rush out my next words: "This is wrong, and you're a bad person," and then make a run for the stockroom before he can respond. Patronizing, thieving jerk.

"Shoshanna!" a voice calls out to me as I rush past the children's section. I spin around to find my boss behind me. Her hair is cropped close to her brown skin, and the turquoise color of her blouse pops against her jet-black power wheelchair.

"Hey, Myra!" I clear my throat. "What's up?"

She tilts her head. "You okay?"

I'm probably flushed from that interaction. "Just some airplane food." That's our code phrase for a bad customer. "I'm okay, though."

"Okay, good." She smiles, and I feel myself relax. I love this woman. She opened Once Upon fifteen years ago. It's the only indie bookstore in Wakesville, Georgia, our midsize city ninety minutes south of Atlanta. Books are basically the best thing to ever happen to anyone ever, so I applied for a job the summer after my freshman year. Myra and I spent the hour-long interview discussing fan theories for our favorite series, Time Stands Still, and just like that, I was hired. "We have a new employee," Myra continues. "He's in the break room, and I need you to show him the ropes, all right?"

"Absolutely, captain!" I salute her.

She shakes her head. "Don't do that."

"Yes, ma'am." I bow.

"Don't do that, either."

"All right, Your Highness." I curtsy.

She points at me and grins. "Now that I like."

I curtsy again and then head to the break room. As I open the door, I cheerfully say, "Hello! Welcome to Once Upon! I'm Shoshanna and today—"

My spiel is cut short when I set eyes on the new hire.

The *hot* new hire.

The *are-you-a-lead-in-a-Netflix-teen-movie* freaking hot new hire.

He's white and has dark brown eyes and hair and a jawline sharper than the edge of our display tables I always bang my legs on. He must go to a different school because I definitely would have noticed him walking down the hallway of mine. Heat rises to my cheeks. How dare someone look so attractive this early in the morning? It's an attack, honestly.

I smile and hope my lipstick hasn't gone rogue and ended up on my skin again. "Hi, hello. I'm Shoshanna!"

"You mentioned," he says.

"Oh, right." I rock back on my heels. "And what's your name?"

"Jake." He stretches, pulling one arm behind his head and tugging it with the other. His flannel shirt rises up a bit, exposing the world's tiniest sliver of skin. I bite my lip. I should get out of this room. This small room with just us inside of it.

"Let's head out to the floor, Jake!" I clap my hands together. "Nothing special about the break room. Whiteboard has our phone numbers and the weekly schedule. Fridge, label your food, but most of us eat in the food court. Bring your own lock for the lockers. And . . ." I pluck a spare name tag off the whiteboard. "Here you go."

His hand grazes mine for a moment, and I squeak and

jump back. He gives me a funny look and then glances at the name tag. "Peeta Pettigrew?"

"A little book humor. We give it to the new people. You'll get one with your own name if you stick around long enough."

"Right," Jake says. He stands and slips the name tag into his pocket.

"Oh, you actually need to wear it!"

"Sure," he responds. But he doesn't move to put it on. Huh, maybe he's team Gale or something.

Now that Jake is standing, I notice he isn't very tall, maybe five-six. But since I'm only five feet, he's probably the perfect height for my head to fit into the crook of his shoulder, which is not at all a weird thing to observe the first time you meet someone. He picks up a spiral notebook from the table, rolls it up like a newspaper, and shoves it into his pocket. "Are you a writer?" I ask. "I like writing too! I'm working on my first book. It's a disaster but not a total disaster, which I think is impressive for my first try!"

"No," Jake replies.

"Real monosyllabic, aren't ya, buddy?"

He just stares at me.

"Not even a single syllable that time!" I wait for a laugh but only get more staring. I tug on the sleeve of my cardigan, feeling a hint of unease. Why isn't he laughing? I'm being funny. "Anyways." I clear my throat. It's fine. Jake probably just has first-day jitters. I'm sure he'll warm up to me soon. "Off to the floor!"

I spin and push open the door. But it doesn't budge because it's the world's heaviest door, and I have the strength of the runt of a hamster litter. There's a button to open the door automatically, but I'm in too deep now to retreat. I push the door again with my shoulder and a huff, but it only cracks open an inch. Then an arm reaches out above me and shoves it open with one solid push, and I'm acutely aware of Jake hovering behind me and how if I leaned back, my shoulders would press against his chest, and my cheeks are heating even more, so I rush out onto the store floor, squeaking out the word "Thanks!"

Jake follows behind me, and I feel in control again. This is my domain. Okay, it's Myra's domain, but I've been working here for a year and a half now, and I'm totally her favorite employee even if she won't say it because favoritism or whatever. I usher Jake around each section of the store, explaining the shelving systems and different tasks he'll need to do. Jake is attentive but silent.

"Myra owns Once Upon," I say as we round the corner to the children's section. It's my favorite part of the store. There are shelves of books I devoured as a child and new ones out all the time. There are little tables and chairs where Mr. and Mrs. Murillo, retired schoolteachers and loyal customers, host story time twice a week. And Myra's husband, an architect by trade and carpenter by hobby, even built a wooden castle for the kids to crawl inside of and read. Sometimes, when I get to work really early, and it's only Myra in her office and me on the store floor, I curl up inside the castle with a good book and soak up the calm.

Yes, I can fit inside a children's wooden castle.

"You met Myra for your interview," I continue. "She's pretty great, as long as you follow shelving protocol. So, like, for example, don't shelve all the purple books together on Prince Remembrance Day, even if she's a huge Prince fan and you thought she'd appreciate it."

Jake raises an eyebrow. "Specific."

"I may or may not be culpable." I catch his eye and try for a grin. He doesn't grin back. The hint of unease grows. "Right," I muster on. "So we all have six-hour shifts, and we can take a half-hour break for food when we want. Like I said, I usually meet my friends at the food court. You could join us today—"

"I brought my lunch."

"Well you could—"

He cuts me off again. "No, thanks."

My back stiffens. I'm getting low-key thieving-jerk-in-the-philosophy-section vibes, minus the thieving. I don't know exactly what's going on here, but I do know this Jake guy doesn't have to be rude. "I'm just trying to be friendly," I tell him.

"And I'm just trying to learn how to do my job."

"Well, part of your job is *being friendly*. Like me."

Jake's response: raising his eyebrows.

I'm about to bite back when a young voice cuts in. "Um, excuse me, miss." I look to my left and see a young girl around eight wearing lime-green overalls. I ignore Jake and his attitude and his jawline and kneel down so I'm the same height as the girl. "Hi there!" I stick out my hand. "I'm Shoshanna. What's your name?"

She shakes my hand with a funny grin, then shyly says, "Marissa."

"Marissa! That's an awesome name." I glance back at Jake. "Isn't Marissa an awesome name?"

I make direct eye contact with his stupid-beautiful brown eyes. A challenge. I bet he can't handle a single customer interaction, especially with a kid. But he surprises me by smiling, and it's a ridiculously good smile that makes me blush, and thank hashem he's looking at Marissa and not me so he doesn't notice. "Definitely an awesome name," Jake agrees. He gives her a thumbs-up, and she giggles and gives him a thumbs-up back. Well, fine. Whatever.

"How can we help you today?" I ask Marissa.

"I want a book," she says. "But I've read all the Princess Doctor ones."

I smile approvingly. Princess Doctor is a series of early readers books about the Princess of Wynthrop, who gets a medical degree and goes around the world saving people.

She's a total badass. "Those are great books! Some of my favorites! You know, I can think of a few other stories you might like. . . ."

Marissa trails me around the children's section as I pluck half a dozen books off the shelves for her. The stack is getting precarious in her small arms when her dad turns a corner and calls her name. She rushes over to him, and he looks aghast at the large pile of books clutched to her chest, but he nods and takes them up to the register. I give a satisfied sigh as they walk away. I seriously have the best job.

Then Jake asks, "So Princess Doctor is one of your favorite books, huh?"

I turn to him and narrow my eyes. "Your tone is *quite* judgmental. Your face is quite judgmental too." His smile is all amused, and *now* it seems like he's about to laugh. Jerk. "Princess Doctor is a fantastic series and feminist as heck. You're missing out." I cross my arms. "Why? What do you read? Great works of *lit-er-a-ture*?"

"I don't read, unless it's for school."

My mouth drops. "I'm sorry, what? You don't read?"

"Nope."

I can hear my voice getting louder. "Then why do you work at a bookstore?"

He speaks the next words slowly and laced with condescension thicker than the philosophy thief. "Because I needed a job, *Shoshanna*."

"Don't talk to me like that. Don't say my name like that."

The dots are starting to connect. No wonder this guy is standoffish. He doesn't read books. He's not even one of us. And he's talking down to me, treating me like I'm silly and naive probably because I like kids' books and chipmunk-print dresses. And it's even worse than that guy in the philosophy section because Jake *works* here. And here, Once Upon, is my second home, a retreat from the rest of the world, a bubble of comfort and security—an escape from closed doors and fighting parents.

And now, Jake threatens to destroy it.

My fingers twitch, automatically grabbing the walkie-talkie hooked to my dress.

"What are you doing?" Jake asks.

I press the PA button. The speakers crackle.

He takes a step forward. "Seriously, what is your problem?"

"Attention," I speak into the radio. "We have a code purple." Jake looks murderous as my voice booms out over the store. "The new hire *doesn't read books*."

Chapter Two

"Did you really just announce that over the store speakers?" Jake asks.

"Do you really *not read books*?"

"I read books. I read them for school."

"Yeah, but you don't read for fun, so what are you doing at a bookstore?"

"*Working,*" Jake says.

"Hey, Shosh! That was an . . . interesting announcement." I spin and find Daniel, my work husband, behind me. Daniel is Black and tall, and when he ran my orientation on my first day, we bonded over our bookish enthusiasm and belief in giving people zero shade for their favorite genre, even if that genre is Loch Ness monster romances. Yes, it's a thing. No, don't google it.

I've always had a little crush on Daniel because he's a book nerd with biceps and I'm a heterosexual girl, but he's been in a relationship since we met, and I can't even begrudge him for it because his girlfriend, Lola, is both the coolest and the sweetest.

"New hire?" Daniel asks.

"Yup," I pop out the word. "Daniel, Jake. Jake, Daniel."

"What's up, man?" Daniel asks. He leans forward and slaps hands with Jake.

"Not much," Jake responds.

"Where's your name tag?"

I bite back a snicker. Okay, I fail to bite back a snicker. Jake does not look amused. "Fine," he says, then pulls the name tag out of his pocket and pins it on.

"Love that thing." Daniel grins. "Peeta Pettigrew. Perfect Harry Potter–Hunger Games crossover."

"Never read them," Jake says.

"Ah," Daniel replies. "So the announcement was true. That's okay. I wasn't a reader either until like ninth grade, and now I'm double-majoring in English and screenwriting." He pauses. "With a minor in poetry."

"Seriously?" Jake laughs.

Daniel nods. "Seriously."

Guilt pinches my stomach. Of course it's okay Jake isn't a reader. I didn't mean it's not okay. Not everyone reads. I only meant it's weird that he works *here* and doesn't read, when there are like a million other stores in the mall.

Suddenly, Myra descends upon us. She zips forward in her chair with intimidating speed, and then stops short in front of me. "Shoshanna," she says, voice firm. "Radio, now."

"Okay, but—"

"*Now.*"

I swallow hard and hand over the radio. Myra presses the PA button. "Attention, Once Upon employees and shoppers, Shoshanna Greenberg has lost radio privileges. You're welcome."

"Now how is that fair?" I ask.

"Because I'm the store owner," she replies. Then she glances over at Jake, who looks quite smug. "I apologize, Jake. I'll have Daniel take over your training."

"Thanks," Jake says.

Daniel pats him on the back. "C'mon. Let's start with the register."

As he leads Jake off, I raise my voice. "Et tu, Daniel?"

He laughs. "Chill out, Shosh. See you later."

Once they're gone, I turn back to Myra. "I'm sorry," I say. "That probably wasn't the most professional announcement in the world."

"Yeah, probably not." She eyes me. "If you want PA privileges, you've got to prove you're responsible enough for them."

"I know." Most employees earn PA privileges after three months. It took me six. For some totally unknown reason, Myra didn't trust me with the power.

"And for the record," she says, leaning back in her chair, "although I love a well-read employee as much as the next person, you don't need to be a bibliophile to stock shelves and ring up customers. It's the holiday season, and Jake came with a great reference."

"But what if someone asks him for a book recommendation?"

"Well, then *you* can help them. Farshteyt?"

"Are you using Yiddish against me?"

"You're the one who taught it to me, mamaleh." Myra's teasing eyes ease the tension in my shoulders. *Yeah, she still loves me.* "Go take your lunch and then come back and do what you do best."

"Enchant people with my dazzling personality?"

Myra rolls her eyes. "Sell books."

"Over there!" I shout, pointing to a table at the back corner of the food court. "Quick!"

"Take my tray." Cheyenne shoves her tray into my spare hand, and as I balance both our lunches, she sprints through the packed food court, diving and diverting around shoppers with dozens of bags and preteens moving in packs. She's almost there when a man with a double stroller barrels her way, but she spins, leaps, and slides into the chair, shoving both her arms over the table. "Goal!" she shouts.

"Success!" I cheer. With our trays, it takes much longer to

thread through the crowd, but eventually I navigate the maze and join her at the table.

"I knew those rhythmic gymnastics lessons would come in handy one day," Cheyenne says as she reaches for her food. Cheyenne has had many enthusiastic but short-lived interests including but not limited to rhythmic gymnastics, French horn, kickboxing, calligraphy, and competitive karaoke. *I must go where my muse takes me*, she declares. I just hope her muse never, ever returns her to fly-fishing because she convinced me to join her once, and gross, freaking gross.

Cheyenne takes a long sip of her milkshake and groans in satisfaction. "Ugh, sweet sustenance, how I needed you. I'm so tired, Shosh. I should've quit before the holiday season started."

"Would your dad have allowed that?"

She pauses before saying, "Probably not."

I love working at Once Upon, but I do also need the job, or I wouldn't have money for gas or car insurance—or, okay, these really cute Harry Potter hairpins shaped like quills. Mama teaches art classes, and Mom is a bookkeeper for a marketing company. We've always had enough but not much more. Cheyenne's parents are well-off for our area. She doesn't need the money, but her dad wanted her to learn the value of a dollar and insisted she get a part-time job.

"At least you don't work with your ex anymore." I shrug. "That was awkward."

"*Yeah*," Cheyenne draws out the word while she plays with her straw. "But, the thing is, I kind of miss Anna."

"What?" I lean forward. "This is new information. When did this happen?"

"Recently. I don't know. I think it's the holiday season." Cheyenne sighs. "Plus, she was, like, a supergood kisser. Folding sweaters is somehow even more boring when you don't have someone to kiss. Shocking, right?"

I laugh and steal one of her French fries. Cheyenne broke up with her girlfriend, Anna, two months ago. I'm not sure why. I'm not a seasoned dating expert. Technically, I've never dated before. And by technically, I mean I've never dated before. Anyway, a couple of weeks after they broke up, they got tired of making awkward eye contact over cardigan displays, so Anna left the Gap and got a job at Nordstrom, which is pretty cool because they never hire high school kids.

"Hey, y'all! What's going on?"

I glance up and find Geraldine standing next to us, holding a tray of chips and guacamole. She's wearing perfectly winged eyeliner and brick-red lipstick. Geraldine and I have been best friends since elementary school. We were the two nerds who always asked our teacher for extra reading assignments.

"Cheyenne's lusting after her ex," I fill her in. "How's work?"

"Ooh, interesting! Scoot," Geraldine orders. I slide over so we can both fit on my chair, one butt cheek each. "Work is hot. Really testing the limits of my waterproof mascara. Feels like I'm never going to save up enough to buy a camera." She sighs and fans her face. "Guacamole anyone?"

"Yes, please!" I snag a chip. Geraldine works at Bo's Burritos and is trying to save up enough to fulfill her dream of becoming a beauty YouTuber. She's honestly destined to be a star. Even back in elementary school she had style, pinning back her tight curls in a new way each day, convincing her parents to let her get lip gloss with color. She's a total van Gogh with a makeup brush and eye shadow palette.

"You *will* save up enough eventually," I say. "And in the meantime, you can practice your artistry on me, okay?"

"Thanks, Shosh." Geraldine grins. "I'll take you up on that. How are things at Once Upon?"

My expression must go sour real fast.

"Holiday shoppers?" Geraldine asks.

"Someone highlight in your favorite book again?" Cheyenne asks.

"Nope," I respond.

"What, then?" Geraldine leans toward me.

I pop a chip in my mouth and crunch hard. "Jake."

Cheyenne narrows her eyes. "Who's that?"

"The new Once Upon employee. I had to show him around this morning, and he's rude as all heck."

Geraldine and Cheyenne exchange smirks.

"What?" I ask.

"By rude . . . ," Geraldine says. "Do you mean he wasn't immediately charmed by you?"

"No!" I shout. "I mean . . . maybe. . . ." I think back on our conversation. Was Jake being a jerk or was I being a bit much? Probably both. But either way, calling him out over the PA system took things too far. I should apologize when I get back to the store.

"Is he cute?" Cheyenne asks, snapping me out of my thoughts.

"Is he, though?" Geraldine chimes in.

I roll my eyes. "Seriously, y'all? Are we not feminists?"

"Please," Cheyenne responds. "Feminism has nothing to do with it. Now, on a scale of one to ten."

"Fine." I look up, as if the answer is written on the ceiling that hasn't been cleaned since this mall was built in the eighties. "He's an eight." But even as I say it, his smile flashes in my mind, and my stomach gets all fluttery. *Damn it.* "Maybe a nine."

Cheyenne whistles.

Geraldine crunches a chip. "Not. Bad."

"TIMOTHY, GET DOWN!" a shouting parent turns our attention to the center of the food court, where a little boy has climbed onto a high-top counter and is chucking Lego pieces at people passing by.

Geraldine blows out a gust of air. "How many more days until Christmas?"

"Six," I answer.

I love the holidays, with all their sparkling lights and delicious baked goods. And I really love helping people find the perfect present because it's a wonderful feeling when you open up a gift and realize a loved one *gets* you. I can't wait for Latkepalooza tonight when my moms will open their presents (carefully curated books, of course). I'm sure our festive Hanukkah celebration will resolve any petty fights.

"It's going to be a long week," Cheyenne says.

"But at least we're here together," Geraldine adds.

We glance around the chaotic mall as that reindeer song plays for the fifth time today, and then we nod in mutual commiseration, holiday soldiers prepped for retail war. I lift my cup. "L'chaim, y'all."

They tap cups and chorus, "L'chaim."

"That will be thirty-eight twenty-two," I say. "Would you like a bag?"

"Yes, please," the woman responds. I slide the three paperbacks into a bag as she pulls out her credit card, but then: "Oh my god! Hi, Amy!"

Another woman gasps and squeezes past the other people in line. "Monica! How are you? How's Rufus?"

Monica tsks. "Not great. He hasn't had a normal bowel movement in weeks. The veterinarian wants us to change foods again. That's a great top, by the way."

"T.J.Maxx," Amy responds.

"But of course!"

"Um, miss," I say, trying to get her attention. There's a line a dozen people deep, and they're all staring daggers at us. "Your card, please—"

She either ignores or doesn't hear me. My eyes focus on the credit card cinched between her two fingers, as she waves her hand around in enthusiasm. "I love that store," she tells her friend. "I found the greatest deal on a purse the other day. Seventy percent off. Clearance section. Total. Steal."

"Ooh, what designer?"

"Excuse me, miss!" I say a bit more loudly. "If I could just grab your card—"

"I'm so sorry about your dog, Monica," Amy continues.

Oy vey. The people in line are shifting forward, ready to stampede if I don't take action soon. This time I say—okay, I maybe shout, "Monica!"

She jerks toward me, looking stunned.

I clear my throat, then smile and lower my voice. "Hi, I love T.J.Maxx too! We all love a great fashion deal! But do you mind sliding your credit card my way? I can finish checking you out, and you and your friend can go chat—" Literally anywhere else. "Over there? By the lovely coffee cart?"

Monica looks startled but hands over her card.

I swipe it, then hand it back along with her bag of books and an over-the-top grin. "Happy holidays, Monica!"

"You mean Merry Christmas," she corrects.

I grin harder. "Sure."

After another hour on the register, someone takes over for me, and I breathe a sigh of relief. I definitely prefer working on the floor. Recommending books is the reason I love this job. It's like a little burst of endorphins every time I help someone scratch their perfect literary itch.

"Hi, Ms. Serrano," I say when I round the corner to the historical fiction shelves. Ms. Serrano is one of our most loyal customers. She retired from her law career six years ago and is in here at least twice a week browsing for new books to devour. "Can I help you with anything?"

"Shoshanna!" She smiles at me, eyes wrinkling. "I wouldn't mind a coffee. Do you know where my mug is?"

"Of course! Be right back." Ms. Serrano is here so often that she has her own mug in the break room. It's white with blue trim, a beautiful, old chipped thing her father brought over from Italy. During my first week of work, I checked out Ms. Serrano on the register and accidentally charged her for an extra book. I noticed the mistake right as she left the store and ran after her, red-faced with embarrassment, scrambling to explain and apologize, worried I'd get in trouble and lose my job.

But Ms. Serrano just patted my arm and said, "You take that extra book, one you like the most, and donate it to the library for me. All right, dear? Have a good day. See you next week."

She is, to put it simply, my favorite customer.

I head to the break room and fill up her cup, black with one sugar, and grab her a biscotti as well. When I return to the floor, I tell her, "I'll be around, so just let me know if you need anything else!"

"Thank you, Shoshanna," she says warmly, sipping her coffee, her eyes already trained back on the bookshelves. Ah, a girl after my own heart.

The store is a mess. But there are only two hours left in my shift, and then Cheyenne will drive me home, and it'll be time for Latkepalooza! I throw away trash left on display tables and scrape gum off the floor. Humans are disgusting creatures. I try to magic eraser a scuffed wall in the children's section—Myra navigates her wheelchair with speed and precision and has on more than one occasion said if her employees employed a little more coordination like herself, they wouldn't always be banging into and damaging her walls with the book carts. I then move from shelf to shelf, straightening books and picking up strays. There's a tourists' guide to Rome chilling on the sci-fi shelves because sure. I grab it and head to the travel section, which is where I find Jake, stocking the shelves with diligent attention.

I clutch the Rome book and watch him for a quiet moment. His hands are steady and purposeful. His brown curls look soft, and I have the disturbing urge to rub my fingers through them. That spiral notebook is still rolled up and sticking out of the pocket of his jeans, jeans that fit *quite* nicely around his behind.

I step toward him. I'm sure he's actually an okay guy. He was overwhelmed on his first day, and I was leading orientation with 100 percent enthusiasm and 0 percent impulse control, and we got off on the wrong foot. I'll apologize, and he'll thank me for being so gracious, and everything will be great. I fluff my own curly hair before chirping out, "Hey, Jake!"

No response. Maybe he didn't hear me.

Though, I've literally never had that problem before.

"How's your first day going?" I ask.

He turns to me then, eyes meeting mine. "You mean before or after you announced to the store I don't read?"

"Yeah, I'm sorry about that," I say. "Really."

He shakes his head as he picks another book off the cart. "I'm surprised Myra didn't fire you. My other boss doesn't put up with juvenile behavior."

"Juvenile." The word hits a nerve, and my skin flushes. I square my shoulders as I reply, "I am not juvenile."

"Yes," he says. "You are."

"Am not!" I shout.

Jake raises an eyebrow.

My cheeks flame red. "Look, just because—"

"Shoshanna," Jake says, and my heart suddenly thumps, because he says my name smooth and slow, the way someone

29

says a name in a movie before that first, perfect, dramatic kiss.

I bat my eyelashes. "Yes?"

"I don't care what you have to say. It doesn't interest me. I'm going back to work."

I gasp. "That is just—you are just—" I narrow my eyes and step forward. Damn it, he smells delicious. Like freaking baked goods. How is that even possible? Does he have a croissant in his pocket? Is that a croissant in your pocket or are you just—

Okay, focus, Shoshanna. "You, Jake," I say, leaning even closer, "are not a nice person."

His eyes flicker, and I inhale sharply.

But then he just shrugs and turns back around, shelving books he doesn't even read. Adrenaline drains fast, and I feel more confused than angry, but then feeling confused makes me angry because Once Upon is my store, my happy place.

And Jake is going to ruin it.

Cheyenne drops me off at four thirty when the sun is already close to setting because winter is the literal worst. I invite her to join us for Latkepalooza, but she has a cello lesson, so she says goodbye and drives off. Cold wind rattles leaves along the driveway and whips against my bare hands and cheeks. I give Barbra Streisand a loving pat and wonder if Eve had a chance to check on her.

I head inside and find the house is empty, which is kind of weird. Mom always works until at least six, but Mama is usually home by now, out on the back porch painting or curled up on the couch with a book or her tablet games. I pull out my phone to check for missed texts but don't see any, so I send one to the group chain asking when they'll be home.

Despite the long day at work, I'm fidgety from my last interaction with Jake. I have shpilkes, as my bubbie calls it—ants in my pants. So I throw my energy into Latkepalooza decorations. I have excellent decorating skills. Myra has seriously upped her window-display game since hiring me.

I grab the Hanukkah paraphernalia from all over the house. Does any Jewish family keep all of their Jewish stuff in one spot? Doubtful. It's like one of our commandments: Thou Shalt Not Keep the Menorahs and Dreidels in the Same Cupboard, and Thou Shall Not Have One Full Box of Hanukkah Candles When You Can Have Four Different Quarter-Filled Boxes Instead.

It takes more than an hour of searching, decorating, and digging old candle wax out of the menorah to get everything in place, but eventually the white-and-blue tablecloth is on the table, the HAPPY HANUKKAH banner hangs on the wall, and my moms' presents are carefully wrapped. Mama never turns down a good Sapphic romance, so I bought her a couple of recent releases. And I know Mom is going to love the boxed set of her favorite mystery writer. She's a mass-market-paperback fiend, and I have to say, cracking a mass-market paperback spine is the single most gratifying pleasure on this planet.

After I'm done with the gifts, I turn to the sack of potatoes sitting on the counter. Hmm. Shredding potatoes is usually Mama's job, and Mom does the frying, but I'm still the only one here. I rock back on my heels as I pull out my phone. No new messages, and it's six o'clock now. Mama should definitely be here, and Mom shouldn't be far behind. I send out another text, and then, feeling a hint of worry, I go ahead and call Mama. It rings and rings, and I think the call is going to voice mail, when suddenly she picks up. "Hey, sweetie!"

"Hey!" I say brightly. "Where are you?"

"I'm sorry, honey. A teacher is out sick, and I have to pick up his classes. I'll be home in a couple hours. You and Mom get started without me, all right?"

"Oh." My throat feels weirdly tight. "Um, Mom isn't here either."

The line beats with tense silence. When Mama finally replies, she sounds funny—forced positivity like the time my elementary school music teacher told me I had a beautiful singing voice even though we both knew that was a lie. "I'm sure she's caught up with work too!" Silence again. "I'll see you in a couple hours. I love you!"

"Love you," I say, before ending the call.

I put my phone down on the table, then twist my fingers together and look around the empty kitchen. It's quiet. Really quiet. This has always been a loud house—dinners together every night, boisterous chatter and laughter, talking over each other to share our story or funny comment first. Loud and warm, just how I like it. But, standing here now, I actually can't remember the last time we had dinner together, and my thoughts wander back to all of those muffled arguments.

We love Latkepalooza. We cherish Latkepalooza. We've celebrated this night together my entire life. But right now I'm alone. And, strangely, I feel like crying. Which is ridiculous. No crying over fried potato pancakes. My moms will be home soon, and everything will be okay. They're busy. And they're just going through a rough patch or something. Everyone's allowed to have a rough patch.

I take a shaky breath, then head upstairs to my room and sit at my desk. I'll work on my book until they get home. There's something undeniably magical about creating. I love falling deep into my own world. I've been writing this book for more than a year now. I'm up to 107 pages of fantasy and romance and time travel, perhaps more than a little influenced by Time Stands Still. It's my favorite series in existence and is about an entire town that gets magically sealed off from the rest of the world, and no one can leave, and no one ages. And now I'm at the scene where my love interests,

Isobel and Henry, finally share their dramatic first kiss.

After scrolling down to the bottom of the document, I rest my hands on the keyboard and stare at the blinking cursor, imagining Isobel and Henry in the town square at dusk, all that romantic tension swirling between them. But as hard as I try, I can't concentrate. I can't lose myself in my fantasy world. All I can do is sit and listen, waiting for someone to come home.

Chapter Three

Iwake up the next morning to light sounds from the kitchen filtering into my room, the kettle boiling and toaster popping. I roll over in bed and rub the sleep out of my eyes. Last night, Mama came home around eight and knocked on my door. She gave me a big hug and apologized and asked if I still wanted to make latkes. But it didn't feel right with just the two of us, and I'd already eaten a microwave burrito because I am a picture of health. We still went downstairs and lit the candles and said the prayer. Then Mama kissed my head and said she'd drive me to work tomorrow before retreating to her room. Usually, I love watching the candles as they burn and drip down to tiny sparks of light, but last night I retreated back upstairs as well and left the menorah flickering alone on the windowsill.

Mom came home another hour later. No knock on my door, no text, no anything. My parents missed Latkepalooza, our annual tradition, and Mom didn't even apologize. A sick feeling sweeps over me as the smell of frying turkey bacon invades my room. What if the closed doors, the muffled voices, the missed dinners are more than busy schedules and dirty dishes?

What if something is actually wrong?

I climb out of bed and shove my feet into my mermaid-print slippers (I bought them for the delightful irony of mermaids having no feet), and then I walk downstairs into the kitchen. It's quiet, no chatter about work gossip, no music playing with Mom singing along impressively in tune, only the low hum of breakfast preparation. Mama sits at the table with a mug of tea and buttered toast. Mom stands by the stove and glances up at me as I walk in. She seems to force a small smile. "Morning, Shoshanna. I'm sorry about last night. Work is crazy this time of year."

"Thanks." I twist my fingers together. "I understand."

Mom flips her bacon, Mama flips a page of her magazine, and I rock back on my heels. The silence makes my skin crawl, and I realize, for the first time in my life, I feel uncomfortable in my own home.

"I got you guys presents!" I say, making my voice more chipper than I actually feel. My phone, gifted to me a couple months ago when my old one kicked it, was my early Hanukkah present, so I'm genuinely not expecting anything in return. "Want to open them?"

"Absolutely!" Mama digs a knife into the butter container,

barely scraping out a small schmear. "We're out of butter."

"And just about everything else," Mom says. "*Someone* was supposed to go to the grocery store."

"*Someone* picked up two extra classes of teaching last night," Mama replies, voice high and clipped.

"Um." I tug on my Star of David necklace. "I'll go get your presents."

"All right," Mom says as she slips bacon out of the pan and directly onto a stack of paper towels. "But quickly, please. I need to get to work."

When no one came home last night, I put the gifts back in my room. Now I rush to grab them, pulse racing as I run upstairs and then back down. Mom is already in the entry-way, coat pulled on, bacon in one hand, and coffee thermos in the other.

"Oh, here," I say, awkwardly grabbing for her thermos and passing over her gift so she can hold it. "Um, oh, I can get that, too." I grab the pile of turkey bacon. It smells like the dictionary definition of mouthwatering, but my stomach feels too constricted to take a slice like I normally would.

Mom unwraps her present and gives a little happy "Oh!" that sounds a bit fake, like when my grandfather bought my grandmother a toaster for her birthday. Because nothing says I love you and respect you like a kitchen appliance. "Great," Mom says, more warmly this time. "I love them. Thank you, Shoshanna."

I tuck a curl behind my ear and smile at her. "You're welcome, Mom."

She puts the box set on the entryway table and then takes back her breakfast. As she's about to walk out the door, she says, "Oh, Eve stopped by yesterday."

Hope wells in my chest. "Really? What did she say?"

"She got Barbra started, but she'll break down again soon without a replacement part. Eve will do the work for free, but the part costs nine hundred fifty dollars."

I hate that my eyes automatically fly to hers, seeking help. Mom shakes her head. "We don't have the money. You'll need to figure this out on your own." She's not being mean. I know we don't have the money.

"Well, we can help a little!" Mama calls out from the kitchen. I glance over to find her standing in the doorway, mug of coffee in hand. "How much was it?"

"Nine hundred fifty," I reply. "But, um, I can take care of it. I'm working double shifts, and—"

"Yes, you can," Mom says. "I don't know why your mama insists on making me play bad cop."

"Alana, come on," Mama replies. "I said we could help her, not that we would pay for the whole thing."

"Oh?" Mom asks, turning to her. "So you want to put no money toward our retirement this month? And then, what, depend on our daughter to take care of us? You don't think long-term, Alex. You never have."

"Really, guys!" I say, my voice so high it almost cracks. "I can take care of it. No problem."

"Great! Good." Mom sweeps forward and kisses me on the head, then leaves the house, the door shutting hard behind her.

Pressure builds behind my eyes, but I push away the urge to cry. It's a car. Just a car. And I understand we don't have the money. I do. I can find a way to pay for the part: $950. It's not a totally impossible number. I have almost $500 socked away in my little checking account, and I'm mostly working double shifts until Christmas. That would put me close, and then maybe I can pick up an odd job, dog sitting or something.

But it's not that—it's not the car, and it's not the money. It's the fighting. Again and again. Over dishes and groceries and broken vehicles. Something is wrong, faulty. I've depended on my moms for my entire life, but now what has always felt solid feels like it might collapse beneath me.

"Hey, sweetie." Mama's voice pulls me back. She's still standing in the doorway, her hesitant eyes appraising me. "Is that my present?"

"Um." I clear my throat and tuck a curl behind my ear. "Yeah."

I hand it over, and she oohs and aahs as she opens it and then hugs the books to her chest. "I can't wait to get into these. Winter is the perfect season for cozying up with a good romance, isn't it?"

"Mm-hmm," I agree.

"And I have a little gift for you."

"Really?" I ask, brightening a little.

"Really, really." Mama winks. "Follow me." She beckons me forward with a crooked finger, and we walk through the living room and out back to the screened-in porch.

It's freezing out here. The space heaters are off, and I'm only wearing my pj's and mermaid slippers. But there, on Mama's easel, in gold lettering and a midnight-blue background, is my present, one of my favorite quotes from *Time Stands Still*:

I fear I will need an eternity to express the vastness of my love for you. Thank goodness, an eternity is exactly what we have.

"It's beautiful," I say, hugging Mama. "I love it so much." Her hair smells good, like her coconut sea-salt shampoo. Mama hugs me back tight, and I inhale.

I arrive at Once Upon early. The all-staff meeting doesn't start for another twenty minutes, but I needed to get out of the house. Despite Mom leaving for work and Mama's gift, tension clung to the walls. Maybe I can fix it, sweep away the small things stressing them out. Like the groceries. I make a note in my phone to run by the store after work. Yes, I'm budgeting to repair Barbra, but I'm a thrifty shopper, and I'm sure a stocked-up pantry will relieve some tension. I smile as I imagine Mama and Mom chatting over a fresh jar of marmalade and a carton of blueberries. I hold on to that image as I walk back to the children's section, the only place large enough for our entire fifteen-person staff to gather.

Even though I'm early, Sophie-Anne and her boyfriend, Arjun, are already here. As always, they're both dressed in a lot of black, metal, and fishnet. He's leaning against a bookshelf, and she's tucked into him, his arm cinched around her waist and playing with her chain belt. Sophie-Anne tilts her head at me and asks, "Why are you smiling?"

I shrug. "I guess I'm just a smiley person?"

She narrows her eyes. "It's weird." Then she glances back at Arjun. "Tell her it's weird, honey."

"It's weird," he confirms with a nod.

I raise an eyebrow. "Y'all have matching tattoos of Hello Kitty with fangs, and you're calling me weird?"

"Yes," Sophie-Anne replies in all sincerity, seeing nothing odd about their taste in tattoos. From the neck up, Sophie-Anne reminds me of Mama, strawberry-blond hair and pale rosy skin. And her voice even has that sweet Southern drawl.

But that's where the similarities end.

Sophie-Anne pulls out a silver Sharpie, grabs Arjun's hand, and begins to draw what looks like a decapitated unicorn on his brown skin. Romantic. I turn away from them and snag a seat at one of the little tables as Daniel walks into the store. I wave him over, then smooth out my polka-dot dress and tug down the sleeves of my cardigan. Daniel gives me an easy grin as he sits next to me, his knees practically hitting his chin in the kid-size chair. "Coffee?" he asks, sliding his cup my way.

"Yes, caffeine always." I pick up the cup. "Is there cream and sugar in here?"

"There is one cream and one sugar."

I wiggle my nose. "Gross. You know three of each is the minimal acceptable amount."

"Right, I'm the gross one." Daniel laughs and takes his cup back. We chat about what we've been reading and the holiday rush and the ridiculously rude customer who had Daniel recommend her books for thirty minutes and then ordered them from a massive online retailer right in front of him. As more people arrive, Daniel glances up, directing his attention at someone else. "Hey, Jake!"

Jake walks toward our table, his brown curls perfectly sleep-rumpled, his jaw arguably sharper than yesterday if that's biologically possible. He grabs the seat next to Daniel, not even glancing my way as he says, "Morning."

He has on jeans and another flannel shirt, this one checkered red and black, like he just came back from a hike in the woods. I catch his eye. "Chop some wood this morning?"

He pauses, confused, then says, "Yeah, actually."

"Wait, really?" I ask.

But then Daniel turns to him and pulls a graphic novel out of his bag. "Here you go. This is the one we were talking about yesterday."

"Cool, thanks," Jake says, grabbing the book.

"It's awesome. You're going to love it. Or not. You know, no worries if not." I stifle back a laugh at the nerdy excitement in Daniel's voice. If there's one thing he loves more than graphic novels, it's introducing people to graphic novels. He leans forward, arms flexing under his Waterston College T-shirt. "Can't wait to hear what you think."

"What book?" I ask, leaning forward as well.

Daniel glances at me with surprise, almost like he forgot I was here. My shoulders tense. Daniel is my friend. Not just my friend—my work husband. Staffing a second holiday season together is basically as serious as saying our vows. But I feel a kernel of unease as he replies, "*Sleepwalker.*"

"Ooh, awesome!" My voice is too high-pitched, too enthusiastic. "What's it about?"

"Actually, I recommended it to you last year. You never read it."

"Oh." The ground feels shaky again, like it did this morning at home. I scratch my neck. "Sorry."

"No worries," he replies, returning to his conversation with Jake.

My gut constricts. I work in a bookstore. I get book recommendations all day every day, and it's my job to be enthusiastic about all of them. Also Daniel literally, and I mean literally, recommends graphic novels in his sleep. His girlfriend, Lola, told me so. And he said "no worries." So I should feel

no worries about forgetting his recommendation. And yet . . .

"Morning, y'all!" Myra calls us to attention. The children's section has filled up. The full staff seems to be here. Myra holds a mug that says BOOK BABE as she speaks. "Thank you for coming in. I know it's early."

"*Very* early," Sophie-Anne says. She inspects her fingernails, which are now covered in silver Sharpie.

"You'll live," Myra responds dryly. She then goes over all of the standard meeting stuff—schedules and shelving systems and an updated return policy, which will hopefully prevent people from returning books they've already read, like you dog-eared the page, and you want a refund? I'm not prejudiced against those who dog-ear, by the way. I believe in a well-placed dog-ear. But you can't return books with bent pages and expect us to think they're unread.

After about ten minutes, Myra says, "And if you haven't met him yet, please be sure to introduce yourself to our newest employee, Jake Kaplan."

Kaplan? I glance back at Jake and his brown curls and wonder if he's Jewish. I touch my Star of David necklace. There aren't many members of the tribe living this far south of Atlanta. It'd be nice to work with a fellow Jew; well, it'd be nice to work with him if we could actually get along.

"And last, I have some exciting news!" Myra announces. Someone coughs, and Daniel nudges my shoulder and rolls his eyes with a grin. Last time Myra had exciting news it was

that we were switching from medium roast coffee to medium dark roast coffee in the break room. She's also someone who describes NPR as *titillating*, but you know, we love her anyway. "We're going to have ourselves a little competition."

"A competition?" Suddenly I perk up. "I love winning things!"

"Who says you'll win?" Daniel asks.

"I have a better chance than you," I reply.

"You don't even know what the competition is," Jake says.

I lean toward him. "Yeah, well, you don't even—"

"Children!" Myra calls, cutting us off. My cheeks flush, and even Jake and Daniel seem embarrassed. We all turn back to face Myra. "The store is packed for the holidays," she continues. "But we have too many browsers and not enough buyers. I figured y'all could use some incentive. Whoever makes the most sales by Christmas will receive a cash bonus of—" She pauses, and darn it if all of us aren't hanging onto her next words. "—two hundred fifty dollars." Adrenaline whistles through my veins. $250 added to my $500 at home added to my next check would be more than enough to fix Barbra. *And* I can buy some groceries tonight, no problem. Moms won't have to argue about it again.

I jump up out of my chair and shout, "I volunteer as tribute! How do I win?"

"You win by selling books," Myra answers. "And, *more*

45

important, by following the competition rules." She pulls her phone out of its holder on her chair and taps the screen. "Those rules are now in your e-mail. Good luck, everyone. May the odds be ever in your favor."

From: *Myra@OnceUpon.com*

To: *Employees@OnceUpon.com*

7:42 a.m.

Morning, team,

Below are the rules for the Bookselling Bonus:

1. *Each employee is assigned a QR code that can be scanned at the register. Please pick up your stack of codes from my office.*

2. *When you hand-sell a book, give the customer a code and ask them to use it at the register.*

3. *Cashiers are not allowed to use their own codes if the customer doesn't have a code. Yes, I will be watching, and you will be disqualified if I see this happening.*

4. *Cashiers must scan the code they are given. No "oops, I forgot." Yes, I will be watching, and you will be disqualified if I see this happening.*

5. *The code will register the sale. We cannot register how many books were sold, so the competition is by customers not number of books.*

6. *Let me repeat that: We cannot register how many books were sold, so the competition is by customers,*

not number of books. If you sell ten books to one person, that's fantastic! It's still one point.

In case you didn't read numbers 5 and 6, it's one point per customer. No exceptions.
The competition ends when we close on Christmas Eve.

From: *Myra@OnceUpon.com*
To: *Employees@OnceUpon.com*
7:47 a.m.
No, you cannot combine your points with another employee.

From: *Myra@OnceUpon.com*
To: *Employees@OnceUpon.com*
7:49 a.m.
No, Sophie-Anne, you don't have to participate.
Participation is optional for everyone.

From: *Myra@OnceUpon.com*
To: *Employees@OnceUpon.com*
7:51 a.m.
No, Arjun, you don't have to participate, either.
Participation is optional for everyone.

From: *Myra@OnceUpon.com*
To: *Employees@OnceUpon.com*
7:54 a.m.
No, I cannot win my own competition.

From: *Myra@OnceUpon.com*

To: *Employees@OnceUpon.com*

7:56 a.m.

ONE POINT PER CUSTOMER.

From: *Myra@OnceUpon.com*

To: *Employees@OnceUpon.com*

7:58 a.m.

Stop e-mailing me and get to work.

Chapter Four

Jake walks out of Myra's office and slides a batch of QR codes into his pocket.

"Huh," I say.

"What?" he asks, pausing a few feet in front of me. He has stubble today, and I have the distinct urge to touch the stubble and see what it feels like because, as previously established, I'm totally a normal person.

Instead, I clear my throat. "You're competing?"

"To win two hundred fifty dollars? Yes, Shoshanna. I'm competing to win two hundred fifty dollars." I bristle as he uses the same patronizing tone as yesterday.

"Right," I say. "Well, good luck. You'll need it since you can't recommend many books."

"Don't worry about me. I'll win customers over with my charming smile."

I roll my eyes. "What charming smile?"

He smiles, and it is indeed a charming white-toothed

smile that lights up his eyes. Between the smile and the flannel shirt he looks like he should be on the front of a *Men's Hiking* magazine with a fishing pole over his shoulder and a golden retriever panting at his side. *Damn you, smile. Damn you, flannel.* I wish Jake had started working here over summer. Maybe he'd be wearing cargo shorts and T-shirts with borderline sexist statements instead, and there's certainly nothing attractive about that.

"Whatever," I say. *Fantastic save, Shoshanna. Real verbal wit.* I move past Jake and into Myra's office. I've always loved her office, cream walls and pastel paintings, artificial plants that look deceptively real. Her shelving units, custom built low so she can reach them with ease, are neatly lined with her favorite books and knickknacks. And there's always a crisp smell from her fresh linen plug in scent.

But Myra, usually relaxed in her domain, stares are her computer with a furrowed brow. "Um," I clear my throat to get her attention. "May I have my codes, please?"

She glances up at me, and after a weighty pause, says, "Yes, but be sure to follow the rules so I don't have to kick you out of the competition for not following them."

"You have nothing to worry about. Promise."

"Oy." She grabs the codes from her desk and hands them over. But really—she doesn't have anything to worry about. I'm going to play by the rules, win this bonus, and fix Barbra. "I need you on inventory. We got a big shipment in this morning, and those display tables need to stay stocked."

"Okay!" I reply. "I'll sell books after. I'll take the lead in no time!"

"I'm sure you will, because you've . . ." Myra clicks around on her computer and then reads, ". . . 'got this in the bag, losers.' That's what you e-mailed the entire staff, right? "

I gasp. "I didn't CC you!"

"She did e-mail that," Jake says, popping his head back into the office.

I stare hate-daggers at him. But I'm not sure they're strong enough, so to make my message clear, I amp them up to abhorrence blades. "To clarify," I say, straightening my shoulders, "I didn't mean 'losers' in the bullying, *you're a waste of space* connotation, I meant 'losers' in the *you're going to lose the competition and I'm going to win the competition* denotation."

"Thanks, Webster's," Daniel says as he passes the office with a stack of journals in his arms, the cute ones with a cat sitting on a tower of books. I was going to buy one, but I guess I shouldn't waste cash on it now. Not that buying a notebook is ever truly wasteful.

"You know what?" Myra asks. "Shoshanna, take Jake with you. Show him the inventory ropes."

I manage to bite back a whiny *why* because Myra is literally only asking me to do my job. "Sure," I answer instead, and then turn out of the office and tug the edge of Jake's shirt. "C'mon, Mountain Man."

"Mountain Man?" he asks.

"Do you have a golden retriever?"

He narrows his eyes. "Huh?"

I sigh and walk past him. "Never mind. Follow me."

We head to the storage room, which is behind the break room, which is fun because you get to walk through an eighty-degree inferno and into a forty-degree freezer. I pull down the sleeves of my cardigan. The storage room has a large garage door that opens up to a back alley behind the mall. Malls are like superboring versions of Disney World. There are all these hidden hallways and alleys shoppers don't know about, a labyrinth designed to keep stores stocked and remove trash without shoppers ever seeing it. Kind of kills the retail buzz if customers know how much waste it takes to satisfy their high.

"Cold." Jake rubs his hands together.

"You could get us coffees from the break room," I suggest.

I expect him to say no, but he surprises me and says, "Good call."

Huh. Maybe things will ease up between us. Maybe we're like archrivals Nathaniel and Rose from *Time Stands Still*, enemies who begrudgingly accept the necessity of their coexistence and become wary friends. Our necessity being unboxing books, not saving our town from a never-ending, encapsulated time freeze.

"Three sugars, three creams!" I call after Jake as he walks

back into the break room. Smiling and humming, I grab a box cutter and open the first shipment, careful not to press too hard and cut through the actual stock. Oh, the books that have been ruined by a box cutter.

Eh. A stack of a *New York Times* bestselling thriller series. No judgment, truly. People love these books. They're just not my favorites. I move on to the next box and the next, revealing more stacks of thrillers and romance bestsellers and Christmas-themed picture books.

Jake returns with two cups of coffee. He passes me one, and I immediately narrow my eyes. "This feels light," I say, and lift the cap to inspect. "Jake, there's only a quarter cup of coffee in here. And it looks black." I take a sip. Bitter as heck. "Are we out of creamer?"

He shrugs. "There wasn't any left."

"Oh, well could you at least put more coffee in here? And sugar, please."

"Sorry, pot was almost out."

I pause. "*Almost* out?" Then I step forward, suspicious, and take his cup out of his hand, feeling the weight of it. "Your cup is full! You could've poured us equal amounts!"

He grabs his coffee back and takes a sip. "Mmm, three creams and three sugars. Extreme choice, but tasty."

"Monster," I hiss.

He grins, teeth flashing bright like a billboard for whitening, before taking another sip. I hope the coffee stains his teeth. "So, inventory. Show me the ropes, boss."

I'm three seconds from smacking the coffee cup out of his hands. But, no. I need to stay focused. The faster we get through this inventory, the faster I can get back to the floor and sell books. A girl's best revenge is winning a $250 cash bonus.

I point to the opened boxes. "Unpack books. Put books on the cart. Check books off the invoice. Wheel books out to the floor."

"Right, sounds easy enough."

Jake puts his coffee down and starts on the heavy lifting, while I open more boxes. After a few minutes of stacking and sorting, the room grows quiet. I can hear him, standing there, not working. I'm bent over a low-lying box, acutely aware of the bent-over part, and grateful I always wear leggings under my dresses in winter.

I straighten up and turn to Jake. "Can I help you?"

"Why aren't you working?" he asks.

"I am working. I'm opening boxes."

"Yeah, but that's the easy part."

Exactly.

"Incorrect," I say. "It takes precise skill to open boxes without damaging the stock. Maybe in a couple months you'll be up for it. If you somehow stick around."

"Oh, I'm sticking around," Jake replies. He's holding seven hardbacks in the crook of his arm. I can only get four in mine. Show-off. He puts them down on a cart and then steps toward me. "Let me open a box."

"No."

"C'mon, Shosh, let me try."

"Don't use my nickname."

He steps forward once more, and I inhale. He smells like baked goods again, all sweet and cinnamony. Is there a sticky-bun deodorant I don't know about?

"Fine. I won't use your nickname." His eyes lock on mine. *"Shoshanna."*

I swallow hard, skin tingling. Yeah, that's worse.

Just to get breathing room, I pass him the box cutter and step back. "Here."

He seems genuinely excited, enthusiasm flashing in his eyes with the cute glee of a Christian kid on Christmas morning. "Press *lightly*," I instruct as he leans over an unopened box. "You want to barely slice the tape, all right? If you press hard, you could—"

"Uh-oh," Jake says. He steps backs and looks at me with a guilty expression.

"Uh-oh?" I ask. "Seriously?" I rush forward and check the box. Please don't be the restock of *Christmas Killings*— they've been flying off the shelves faster than fictitious serial killer Karl Kringle can murder yuletide lovers. But no, it's not *Christmas Killings*. It's another box of picture books, and they aren't damaged.

Jake smirks. "Got ya."

A murderous feeling floods through me, and I'm super glad he's holding the box cutter so I don't become a butcher like Karl Kringle. Breathing hard, I lock eyes with Jake and calmly say, "Put these on the cart."

"That's it?" he asks. "No yelling?"

I shrug. "I'm more mature than that."

His eyes widen a bit in surprise. "Okay."

Jake unpacks the box, and as quietly as possible, I pick up his coffee cup from the floor behind him and then walk over to the trash can at the other end of the room. "Hey, Jake," I say.

He spins around, eyes on me and then the cup. "Don't—" He tries to stop me.

I smile as I dump his coffee in the trash.

"I might be claustrophobic," I tell Geraldine as we squeeze through hordes of shoppers. Every hallway is clogged with foot traffic, and there are so many big sweaters and stuffed shopping bags and blinking decorations I can barely see straight. I press my arms together, trying to make myself as small as possible so the people barreling past don't knock into my shoulders.

"I didn't know this many people still shopped at the mall," Geraldine replies. She only started working here last summer, so this is her first time experiencing the mad holiday rush. "Don't they know the Internet exists?"

"It's DD Week."

"DD Week?"

"Delayed Delivery Week," I explain. "As in, there are so many deliveries being made, your favorite online retailers can no longer offer two-day express shipping. If people want their gifts in time, they have to buy them in person."

"Ooh, they're in!" Geraldine squeals as we arrive at Make You Up. I'm on a midmorning break with her before she heads into work for the Bo's Burritos lunch rush. I'm going to sell an absolutely epic number of books this afternoon, but first I could use a quick breather from the store—and from Jake—to get into the right bookselling headspace. A little best friend time should be just the fix I need.

Geraldine presses close to the window, her eyes feasting on a display of winter lip kits. "They're gorgeous! I'm in love!" Her giddy enthusiasm is infectious and almost tricks me into caring about winter lip kits. She's going to be a fantastic beauty vlogger. She can sell product with a single squeal!

We walk into the packed store, and Geraldine takes my hand to lead the way. Customers are crammed into every narrow aisle, and the line for the register is *20 Leagues Under the Sea* deep. Even during the holidays, Once Upon never sees this kind of traffic. Maybe we should start selling lotions and face masks along with our copies of *The Silence of the Lambs*.

"Elliot!" Geraldine says.

Elliot spins toward us and grins. His brown hair flops

close to his perfect brows, and he's wearing a Paladin High School football shirt under his store apron. He strides forward and grasps Geraldine's forearms. "Have you seen them?"

"Mm-hmm!" Geraldine responds, eyes alight with true lipstick love. "But not up close."

"Come on, then." Elliot shepherds us over to the lip kits. "Excuse me, pardon me," he says to everyone in our path. "Store emergency. Out of the way."

I laugh. "Your manager must love you."

"Oh, she despises me," Elliot replies. "But I sell more product than any other employee on this floor, so she keeps me around. How's the holiday season at Once Upon?" He grabs two lip kits and hands them both to Geraldine. Elliot knows my makeup routine doesn't get much more advanced than drugstore mascara and lipstick.

"Busy!" I answer, though now that I'm thinking about it, things feel less hectic than last year. I'm probably just older and wiser and faster on the register. "Any books you want for Christmas? I can use my discount!"

"Isn't there a new Aaron Rodgers memoir?"

"Is that a football thing?" I ask.

"Yup!"

I make a face. "Gross. Boring."

Elliot grins. "I've got to work out *and* study up if I want to make varsity next year. At least my growth spurt came just in time." He steps forward and bops me on the head from almost a foot of height above me.

I hear a soft cry next to me and turn to see tears on Geraldine's face as she stares at the lip kits. "Oh, sweet thing," I say. "Are you crying right now? Over *lipstick*?"

Geraldine blinks up at me. "It's not lipstick," she says. "It's limited-edition winter lip kits in Bruised Kiss Burgundy and Punch Me Plum."

"Bruised Kiss? Punch Me Plum?" I raise an eyebrow. "I think there's something wrong with this company."

"They're both gorgeous," Elliot tells Geraldine. "But I think Bruised Burgundy is the winner if you have to choose."

"Choose? I can't even afford one." Geraldine's lips twist. "I'm trying to save up for a camera so I can film on something other than my phone, but then, what's the point if I don't have the makeup to talk about? Some beauty influencers have a dozen new products each week. My favorite, Lucille Tifton, posts a new video *every day*. I'll never be able to compete. . . ."

My heart aches for Geraldine. She's been working so hard to make her YouTuber dream come true. The only reason she works at Bo's Burritos (*an insult to my mother and Mexican food everywhere, though the guac is straight-up delicious*, as she's said) instead of Make You Up is because she gets tips at Bo's, so in the end, she earns more per hour. I don't know how I can make her dream happen, but I do have an idea of how to brighten her day.

As Geraldine stares at the lip kits, I lean into Elliot. "Hey friend," I whisper. "Aren't there, like, samples or something you can give her?" I bat my eyelashes. "Pretty, pretty please?"

"You're real cute," Elliot says.

I beam. "Totally agree."

He pauses for a moment, thinking. "Tell you what. Someone returned a broken tube of the Punch Me Plum earlier today. I'll, um, say it got tossed in the trash by accident. Be right back."

While Elliot searches, I look around the store. Lipsticks and eye shadows sit like jewels in their cases, shining under the store lights. Customers run polished fingernails over tubes of mascara and pots of moisturizer, while other shoppers dust their skin with shimmery powders. A turquoise eyeliner catches my attention, and I immediately think of Mama. She loves mixing it up with funky colors every now and then. I snap a picture and text it to her, along with the message: Super cute, right? Do you have this color?

I need to save my money, but maybe it's on sale, and I can get her a bonus Hanukkah gift. I wait for her to respond, knowing she's more attached to her phone than most of my friends, but I don't get a reply. And then Elliot is back. He discreetly slips the tube to Geraldine and kisses her on the cheek. "It'll look great on you."

"Thank you," Geraldine whispers, staring in reverence at the matte black tube. "Free chips for the rest of your life, okay?"

"Deal!" Elliot says. "I've got to get back to work. Visit again soon, all right?"

"Obviously!" Geraldine replies.

"I'll look for that football book for you," I promise him.

As we head out of the store, Geraldine stares at her new lipstick, eyes mesmerized. "I'm so happy," she says. "Thanks, Shosh."

I lean into her, my heart lifting. "I'm so happy for you."

My phone buzzes, and my spirits lift even more. Mama must have texted me back. Hopefully the eyeliner doesn't cost as much as those lip kits because I really don't have time this week to sell a kidney on the black market. But it's not a text. It's just an alarm reminding me to get back to work.

That's okay. Time to focus. Sell books, win the money, and fix Barbra.

I crack my knuckles. And, as a bonus, show Jake Kaplan where he can shove it.

The rest of the morning and the early afternoon rush by in a blur. I jump from customer to customer, chatting, charming, and generally hand-selling my arse off, not letting anyone even think of leaving the store without a book. My stack of QR codes dwindles so low that I have to pick up a second batch from Myra, who looks *quite* impressed. This competition will be a breeze. No one wants the bonus as badly as I do, and even if they did, definitely no one can sell books as well as Shoshanna Greenberg.

Just now, I have my next victim in sight.

And by "victim," I mean "lucky person about to receive excellent service."

I don't jump on customers the second they walk into the store. That's too aggressive, especially since our clientele lean toward the introverted. A simple *Welcome, let me know if you need anything* is okay but nothing more assertive than that. Book lovers adore a nice, silent browse, and I'm not out here to ruin that for anyone.

But this guy has been staring at the same adult fiction shelf for a full three minutes, and he looks perplexed. Like his brow is literally furrowed. It's officially time for friendly interference.

"Hi!" I smile as I approach. "Can I help you?"

My smile brightens when I notice the guy is my age and more than a little cute. He's tall and has thick blond hair. Blond normally isn't my thing, but he kind of looks like the golden-haired bladesmith in *Time Stands Still*, so it's working for me.

"Ah, sure, thanks!" the guy answers. He gives me a once-over, and I twirl my hair without an ounce of shame.

"Are you looking for anything specific?" I ask, while noticing Jake hovering nearby, probably pretending to straighten shelves while stealing bookselling tactics from the master. Good. Let him experience my brilliance.

"Yes, I'm looking for this book . . ." The guy trails off and runs a hand through his hair. His beautiful, shiny blond hair. Is he as caring and strong as the bladesmith Bryant? Can he carry an injured female warrior, decked in her armor, on his back for a full day and night?

Okay, focus, Shoshanna. This is about a sale, not about flirting. I tilt my head to the side and play with the chain of my necklace. Maybe a little flirting.

"Mm-hmm," I say. "What's the title?"

He shakes his head. "Can't remember. Sorry."

"That's all right! Who's the author?"

"Afraid I don't know that, either."

My smile falters, just for a second. "Okay, no problem at all!"

Out of the corner of my eye, I notice Jake holding back laughter. My neck heats, but I soldier on. This isn't the first time this has happened, and it won't be the last. "What's your name?" I ask.

"Ryan," he answers with an easy grin.

Ryan. Oh my god. So close to Bryant. "*Ryan*, do you remember what the book is about? Or perhaps what the cover looks like?"

There's an elongated pause and an intense facial expression, like he's calculating the propulsion needed to launch a shuttle into space. Finally, he looks back at me with yet another easy grin. "Blue?"

"Right." I clear my throat. "Blue."

"Maybe blue."

My jaw tightens. "Okay. Maybe blue. And is it fiction or nonfiction?"

He stares at me blankly.

It's amazing how quickly attraction to someone can evaporate.

At that exact moment, Jake steps forward and stands in front of me, essentially hiding my entire five-foot frame from Ryan's view. "Hey." Jake throws out his hand for a shake. "I'm Jake. Nice to meet you, man."

I shove Jake's elbow to make room for me by his side. "His name is Ryan," I mutter as they shake hands.

Jake ignores me. "So is this book a real story or one someone made up?"

"A real story!" Ryan answers, eyes lighting up with the enthusiasm of a Labrador retriever setting sight on a tennis ball. "About President Jimmy Carter."

"Fantastic!" Jake claps Ryan on the back. "So we'll head over to the biography section. If you'll follow me . . ." Jake freezes. "Um . . ."

I turn to him and bat my eyelashes. "Something wrong there, Jake?"

When his eyes lock with mine, I feel a spark in my stomach, but I keep my shoulders squared. "Yeah," he mutters. "Where's the biography section?"

I press a hand to my chest. "Oh, do you need my help?"

"Shoshanna."

Why does he have to say my name like that? Almost in a growl. I swallow hard and try to collect myself, but then Jake is looking past me. "Hey, Daniel!" he calls out. "Help me for second, yeah?"

"Sure thing!" Daniel strides toward us. "Heya, Shosh."

"Daniel," I reply curtly. And then before I can stop it, all three guys walk off to the biography section without me. My *sale* walks off without me. I let out a tense breath. *Damn you, Jake Kaplan.* It's not like he has a chance of winning this competition, but stealing a sale might hurt my odds against someone else, might threaten my chance of fixing Barbra.

"Tough luck," a voice says.

I startle and then spin around to find Sophie-Anne leaning against an endcap of science-fiction novels. "Have you been here the whole time?" I ask.

She loops forward and clasps a hand on my shoulder. "What *is* time?" Then she drifts away, long black skirt billowing out behind her.

"Right," I mutter, turning around. "Well, at least she isn't my competition."

"Are you talking to yourself?"

I glance behind me. Sophie-Anne is back. I give a stiff smile and walk away.

* * *

The food court is way over capacity, every table and chair taken, lines so long they're definitely breaking fire codes, people jammed into every corner and crevice as Christmas music competes with their raucous voices. My skin itches. Ugh, people. Don't get me wrong—I like *some* people, but massive crowds of strangers? No thanks.

"Let's get smoothies," Cheyenne says, taking both my hand and control of the situation. "Looks like the shortest line. Probably because it's thirty-three degrees outside."

"Um." I hold us back for a second. "I've got to save up money to fix Barbra, but I can wait in line with you?" I'm planning on a lunch of tea and biscotti in the break room, plus one of the granola bars I always have stuffed at the bottom of my tote bag.

"Oh, no worries," Cheyenne says. "I'll buy you one."

"No, that's okay. You don't have to."

She gives me a look. "It's seriously no problem, Shosh."

I relent with a small smile, and we get in line and place our orders. Cheyenne hands over her card like it's the easiest thing in the world. "Thanks," I say, twisting my fingers together. It's strange, having a friend with more money than you. I wish I wasn't aware of it—I wonder if she's aware of it. I guess I'm more focused on money than usual with the stress of saving up for Barbra. I don't want her repair to be the source of more fighting at home.

I inhale and then breathe out slowly as we grab our

smoothies, mine banana mango tango, Cheyenne's triple berry blast. We walk around the mall since there's nowhere to sit. I must not be holding my shoulders in close enough because a woman carrying a dozen shopping bags barrels past us, bumping my arm hard and almost throwing me and my banana mango tango to the floor. She doesn't even pause to apologize.

"Rude!" I shout, rubbing my arm.

"You okay?" Cheyenne asks. For some strange reason, the question makes my eyes water. I wipe at them, embarrassed. "Hey." Her voice softens. "What's going on?"

I fidget with my straw, throat too tight to take a sip. "It's nothing."

"Shosh," Cheyenne says in her warning tone.

I'm just being sensitive. Like, seriously, who cries because someone bumped into their shoulder? And who gets upset because their friend bought them a smoothie? And yeah, my moms missed Latkepalooza, and that's not a great feeling because it's a night we've celebrated together my entire life, but they missed it to work at their jobs, so there's no reason to be all emotional about it. And mentioning any of this to Cheyenne would make it a thing, and it's definitely not a thing.

"Shosh?" Cheyenne prods again, her warm eyes zeroed in on me. She's wearing an oversize knit sweater today, the sleeves so long they cloak her fingers as she holds her smoothie.

"It's nothing," I say quickly, and then smile. It's a genuine smile—just knowing my friend is there for me if I want to talk means the world. "I promise. Ooh, look, Santa's Workshop!"

Cheyenne accepts my subject-change with a chipper shout of "Santa!"

"You do know Santa isn't real, right?" I ask. "I've accidentally broken that news to so many gentiles over the years. Maybe that's why people hate Jews."

Cheyenne snorts. "Ha, ha. Of course I know he isn't real. But it's fun to see the kids all happy before the harsh realities of the world are shoved in their faces. C'mon. Let's watch."

I glance at my phone. "Okay, but then I've got to head back to work." I still have fifteen minutes left of my break, but if I get back early, that's fifteen extra minutes to sell more books. I bet I'm way in the lead but no harm in getting way, way in the lead.

"How are things going with Jake?" Cheyenne asks as we walk over to Santa.

Jake. Jake the jerk with his stubble and flannel and freaking baked-goods aroma. "Not great," I reply. "He's kind of an ass."

"But he's got a good ass, right?" Her suggestive tone makes my skin flush.

"How would you know?" I raise my eyebrows. "You've never met him."

She smirks. "I can just tell by the way you talk about him."

"*Oh my god*. Please stop," I say.

But, the thing is, she's not wrong.

Cheyenne laughs and wraps an arm around me. We make it to the outside of the line, which zigzags through the better half of the north wing. Kids shout and scream while parents scroll on their phones. The music blasts even louder here, currently playing Mariah Carey's "All I Want for Christmas Is You." This song always gives me the urge to watch *Love, Actually*, which always makes me wish there were also an epic Hanukkah romance movie.

I look toward the stage and see it's blanketed in fake snow and decorated with a red sleigh and reindeer and a sign for the North Pole. It's really quite cute. There are even two elves! And Santa is laughing a jolly laugh, and he . . . huh. Santa looks familiar, brown skin and warm eyes I'd recognize anywhere—

"Oh. My. God." I hold a hand over my mouth so I don't break into hysterical laughter.

Cheyenne stares in shock.

"Is that—" A snort of laughter breaks out despite my most valiant efforts.

She holds up a finger. "Do not."

"But is that—"

"Stop. Talking."

"Cheyenne, is that your dad?"

"Oh my god." Cheyenne shoves her face in her hands

and groans so loudly a couple of parents in line turn and stare at us. Her voice comes out with the dramatic delivery of an actress performing her Oscar-winning role. "How could he do this to me?"

I'm full-out laughing now. Cheyenne shoots me a death glare, and I try to tamp down the giggles. "Well, to be fair," I say. "I don't think he's doing it to you. C'mon, look how adorable he is with those kids! This is the best!"

"Ho, ho, ho!" Mr. Herman bellows. Cheyenne groans louder. Two kids stand before him, beaming up with grins of wonderment. An elf snaps the picture, and then another elf ushers the happy kids off the stage.

Cheyenne moans. "This is so embarrassing."

"No it's not," I say. "It's great! Let's go say hi!"

"We are not—"

But I'm already tugging Cheyenne's arm and walking around the side to the front of the line. "Mr. Herman! Mr. Herman!" I call out, waving my free hand. Mr. Herman, as Santa, looks over in a panic, and I realize I've almost blown his cover. "I mean, Santa! Look! I have your favorite elf here!"

Mr. Herman catches on quickly. "Ho, ho, ho! My favorite two elves here for a visit. Come over and—"

"Nope!" Cheyenne shouts, spinning around and dashing away from the North Pole. I chase after her, almost knocking into a trio of preteen boys on skateboards in the sardine-packed mall, as Cheyenne continues to say, "Shoshanna, it's my dad.

Dressed as Santa. Saying 'ho, ho, ho.' Oh my god. What if Anna sees him? This is too embarrassing. I can't—"

I feel the tiniest twinge of annoyance as she speaks. Mr. Herman was so happy to see his daughter. He wanted Cheyenne to spend time with him. My moms were ecstatic when I got my job at Once Upon. They showed up at the end of my first shift with a tray of rainbow-frosting cupcakes to share with the entire staff. It was too dang nice to be embarrassing. After that, they'd drop in on random occasions to browse, buy gifts, or treat me to lunch at the food court. All these little things I loved but never thought about much. Now, it would feel surreal to see Mama bringing me an Auntie Anne's pretzel or to find Mom trailing her finger along the spines of the mystery section.

But it's not right to be annoyed at Cheyenne when I haven't told her what's going on at home. And, to be fair, I've never witnessed my moms in elf costumes. That might be a sight I couldn't recover from.

As we head back toward our respective stores, Cheyenne pulls out her phone and calls someone. A few seconds later she breathlessly says, "Mom? Yeah, hi." Her eyes are wide and wild with panic. "There's an emergency."

Chapter Five

For the next few hours, I lose myself to bookselling, racking up sale after sale, peddling five copies of the first Time Stands Still book alone, not to mention plenty of memoirs, romances, and adorable picture books. My own to-be-read pile has grown to Jack-and-the-Beanstalk heights, and I can't wait for these holiday double shifts to be over so I have more time to actually read.

After helping another customer, I look around the store and sigh in contentment. I freaking love my job. People enter Once Upon hesitant, hopeful, eyes flitting across the shelves in search of something special, and I get to help them. I get to comb the shelves and come up with the right title to brighten their entire week or even year. There's nothing quite like the perfect book—nothing else in the world that can shine a light on something deep down inside of you, that can burrow into your heart and make you feel seen and heard. Holiday bonus or not, finding that perfect book for someone is a greater burst of adrenaline than even my most legendary sugar rush (Halloween, 2016).

I notice Daniel is finishing up with a customer as well, pointing them over to the registers with a pleasant smile. I size him up with sudden suspicion. *Daniel*, reader of all the books, speaker of countless recommendations, wearer of Spider-Man socks. He's one of the few employees in the store more well-read than me and just as personable. If I have competition for the bonus, he's it. And just because we're nerdy BFFs who once came up with 101 alternate titles for the Harry Potter books together (including *Harry Potter and the Goblet of Teenage Angst* and *Harry Potter and the Deathly Angst*), it doesn't mean I'll go easy on him.

Daniel notices my gaze and laughs as he approaches me, running a hand over his hair. "You should see the look in your eyes. If I didn't know better, I'd be scared of you, Shoshanna Greenberg."

"So . . . ," I say. "Planning to win the bonus?"

He winks. "Subtle. But don't worry. I'm not working enough shifts to win. Family is in town early for Christmas, so I won't be pulling doubles like you."

"Oh, good," I say, feeling quick relief.

Daniel laughs again as his phone chimes. He checks it and says, "Ah, Lola is here. I'm heading out." He salutes me. "See you later, Greenberg."

I salute back. "Until tomorrow, Rhodes."

He walks away, sliding his phone into his pocket and high-fiving Myra on the way out, and a little sigh escapes me. Not to be all cliché or whatever, but it'd be nice to have *someone* during the holidays. Daniel has Lola, and it's totally understandable why Cheyenne is all lustful after her ex, Anna. Who doesn't want to cozy up with someone during the cold weather? Of course it's at the exact moment of that thought that I look up and find Jake standing in the adult fantasy section. He's talking with a customer, laughing and running a hand through his luscious head of curls. I bite my lip as my eyes flicker from his jaw to his flannel all the way down to his brown boots, and I wonder for just a moment . . .

But then the laughing stops. And Jake looks awkward, and the customer gives a *This guy is no help* sigh. So in a burst of holiday goodwill, and definitely for no other lustful reasons, I decide to lend a hand.

I walk over and keep my voice bright as I ask, "Can I help you find something?"

"I've got it, thanks," Jake answers.

I step up to him close enough to whisper, "Just let me help." When he looks at me, I almost wobble backward. His dark brown eyes are intense, "swoonworthy," some might say, and up close they make my head light, my thoughts slow yet heady, like I just downed two glasses of wine at a seder. I manage, *barely*, to keep my voice level as I tell him, "You can keep the sale."

Those swoonworthy eyes narrow as he scratches his neck with two fingers. I find myself staring at the soft patch of skin a second too long. "Really?"

I clear my throat and flick my eyes back to a safe area—also known as a piece of lint on my cardigan sleeve. "Really," I promise. "I kicked bookselling butt this afternoon. It's not like an extra sale will bring you anywhere close to beating me."

"Fine," he relents, and I swear I sense a small grin tugging at his lips. "Okay, then."

My pulse ticks faster than usual. I really did step up close to Jake, close enough I can feel the warmth of him through my cardigan and his flannel. My cheeks heat as I turn to the woman standing in front of us and focus my attention on her instead of Jake and Jake's *warmth*. She's holding a stack of three books, but her frown tells me she's unhappy with the choices.

I stick out my hand. "Hi! I'm Shoshanna. Can I help you find something?"

She shifts the books and shakes my hand. "I'm looking for a gift for my dad. He likes fantasy, and I want to get him something recent, written by a woman, if possible."

"Oh!" I say. "He *has* to read Time Stands Still. It's the best series to—"

She shakes her head. "No, I want something recent."

"It's recent!"

She gives me a weird look. "Didn't that series end, like, a decade ago?"

Well, in the history of literature, I'd still call that pretty dang recent, but the customer is always right, especially when I'm showing Jake the definition of exemplary customer service, and I'm still *very* aware of Jake at my side. "Right! Okay, so we have a display table of new fantasy. Let's see if any of those are the right fit!"

I try to lead her off to the display, but she stays put. "Anything you'd specifically recommend?"

"Every single one is a staff recommendation!" I assure her, finally ushering her over to the table. Jake trails behind us, and we all pick through the titles together. Now that I'm looking at the display, I realize I haven't read any of these. I love fantasy. It's basically my favorite genre, but I guess I'm a little behind, which can happen when you reread your favorite series approximately eight times in a row and also read assorted fanfiction for that series. I feel the woman's hesitancy and hate the discomfort of not having an immediate solution. I rack my brain, but every title that comes to mind was released at least a few years ago.

"So something like *Time Stands Still* but recent?" Jake asks.

"Exactly!" the woman replies.

"It's a great series," Jake says.

Oh, come on. He hasn't read it.

"One second . . ." Jake pulls out his phone, and after a

minute of typing and tapping, he says, "How about Elyse Greene's Willow Warrior series?"

"Have you read it?" she asks.

"Not yet," he responds, "but I'm planning to soon. It's on a list of recently released reads for fans of Time Stands Still."

She claps her hands together. "Oh, that's perfect!"

Anxiety pulses through me. Can Jake really sell books that way? With lying and a smartphone? What if it's a good strategy? What if he wins the bonus, and I don't have enough money to fix Barbra, and my moms will keep fighting about it, and—

Before I can stop myself, I'm saying, "Oh, I know exactly where that one is! Follow me!" I spin on my heel and lead the woman back to the fantasy shelves. I find the book and pass it over, along with my own QR code. "Just hand this in up front, thanks so much. Happy holidays!"

After the woman heads to the register, Jake walks up to me, jaw tense, swoonworthy eyes now alight with annoyance. "Seriously? You said that was my sale."

His words hit harder than expected, and my shoulders tighten. I *did* say that was his sale. I just got anxious and panicky about losing the bonus. "You're right," I admit. "I'm sorry. But you also basically stole my sale this morning with Ryan the Jimmy Carter fan. So. We're kind of even."

"Oh." Jake's expression flickers. He leans closer to me, and I inhale all his sugar-and-cinnamon scent like he's a life-size bowl of Cinnamon Toast Crunch. "Yeah, well, I guess you're right. I'm sorry too."

The moment stretches too long, and my skin buzzes, all electric and hypersensitive, like I can feel Jake even though we're not touching. My eyes flick to the curve of his lips, and the electricity grows, and I worry if one of us doesn't speak soon, I'll do something *extremely* regrettable. So I clear my throat and say, "It's not like it matters. You're not going to win the bonus."

"You really think I can't win?" Jake leans back and stretches, pulling one arm tight across his chest. He seems more amused than annoyed now. "Because I found that woman a book just now—not you."

"It was a fluke," I tell him and myself. "You can't google up a perfect recommendation every time. People want a personal touch. They want you to vouch for a book."

"Which is something you couldn't do. Besides, people like search-engine-optimized results. They want to be led to exactly the right choice." Jake's expression shifts then, and he gets this evil smirk that makes my hairs raise.

"What?" I ask.

"Nothing."

"Jake . . . ," I warn.

His smirk intensifies. "You know what? I'm going to straighten the shelves. The next customer is all yours. I'm sure you're right. It'd be the upset of the century if I win the bonus."

As he walks away, I call after him in a panic, "Why were you smiling when you said that? Jake!"

He doesn't answer.

Darn it.

Why was he smiling when he said that?

I bite my nail as the Starbucks' line inches forward. I'm overreacting. I know I'm overreacting. Jake can't win the bonus. He's messing with me, that's all. And I'm being sensitive. I've always been a little sensitive. I once cried at a commercial for a carpet cleaner because the family was just *so happy* to have that new puppy, muddy paws and all. And the tension at home and Barbra's impending breakdown is making me more on edge than usual, and why am I about to waste money at Starbucks when I didn't even want to buy a smoothie, like what's the point of a pick-me-up when there's so much stress attached to it, and I just feel like one more tiny thing could topple me over, and—

I exhale a giant, shaky sigh.

"Whoa, what's up with you?" a voice asks.

I spin around, muscles tense, but then relax when I see who it is. "Elliot!"

"I need caffeine," he says. "This day has been way too long."

"Agreed." I smile. "The crowds at Make You Up looked intense."

"So intense. It's all hands on deck for the holidays, and

I want to be seen as helpful since I'm trying to get a raise from Kim. Seriously, I sell twice as much product as anyone in that store, but she won't give me a raise because I have a problem 'listening to authority,' or whatever. And yet she seems to have no qualms about having me close down the store tonight, and—"

"Wait!" I interrupt, an idea sparking. "You're closing the store tonight?"

Elliot sighs as he runs his fingers through his perfectly tousled hair. His silver rings glint under the mall lights. "Yeah. Kim has to leave early for some hot yoga acupuncture meditation cult thing. I don't know."

"Hmm," I say.

An entirely empty store full of makeup . . .

"You have something brewing in there." Elliot taps my forehead. "Tell me!"

"Well . . . if you're closing down the store, you know, the store with all the makeup, what if we film Geraldine's first video there using the samples? Oh my god!" I jump. "I can even borrow a backdrop from an old event at Once Upon, so no one will recognize where we are. It's totally seriously perfect!"

"I'm intrigued. But sounds risky." We step up to the cashier, and Elliot orders. "Two grande peppermint mochas, please!"

"That'll be eleven seventy-four," the cashier says.

I freeze. I should split the cost, but he's the one who ordered us something expensive when I was already feeling guilty about my plan to order a kid's hot chocolate. Before I have a chance to react, Elliot inserts his card, and the cashier hands him a receipt.

"I'll get us next time!" I say. "Promise."

"Sounds good," Elliot replies, totally unconcerned. I chew the inside of my cheek as we step to the side to wait for our drinks. "So, a video . . ."

"Yeah. What do you think? No pressure, though. I don't want to get you in trouble!"

"I think . . ." Elliot trails off into a long pause before smiling at me. "I think it's a fantastic idea, and I'm very much in!"

I squeal. "Really?"

"Really, really."

And just like that, a giant weight lifts from my tiny shoulders. Helping Geraldine will be the perfect way to make her YouTuber dream come true, and as a bonus, distract me from any future stress spirals.

When our drinks are ready, I grab mine and take a sip. Pepperminty, chocolatey perfection. "I should head back to work," I tell Elliot.

"Text coordinate details?" he asks.

"For sure!"

He gives me a quick, one-armed hug before we part ways. The shoppers quickly disappear him into the crowd. As I sip my drink, I pull out my phone and text Geraldine about tonight. She immediately sends back a slew of texts, mostly excitement with a medium dose of nerves. She says she's not ready to post content online but that she'd love to do a practice video. Happiness floods through me as I sip my peppermint mocha and head back to Once Upon. I'm bolstered by sugar and friends and ready to sell a lot of freaking books.

Chapter Six

Jake leaves halfway through my double shift, so the rest of the day goes by without incident. Well, there are customer incidents. Like the customer who insists on only *boy book* recommendations for her son and scoffs, literally scoffs, when I hand her a book with a girl protagonist. And then there's the ten-minute-long, painstaking conversation I have with a customer who said he preordered a book for pickup on Wednesday and why isn't it here yet, and I said yes, well, it's only Monday, and he said, yes, but I ordered for pickup Wednesday, and I barely resisted the urge to scream, *That isn't how time works, sir!*

But, you know, that's just retail life.

And then my period started, and I didn't have a tampon on me, so I borrowed one from Tanya, a mother of two who carries everything from tampons to graham crackers to Tide to Go pens on her at all times. She's such a good person she'll probably even carry around an emergency tampon for other people once she's post-menopause. I make a mental note to bring her some packets of chamomile tea since it's her favorite, the break room is always out of it, and it seems to be the one thing she can't fit into her Mary Poppins bag.

The afternoon wasn't all bad, though. I sold an obscene amount of books, and even better, Ms. Serrano and I had a thirty-minute chat about a new romance series she loves, and then she gifted the books to me because she said they're going to put her on that *Hoarders* show if she doesn't start purging her personal library. And now it's finally the end of my shift, and after two days of double shifts in a row, I'm bone tired, which is an expression my grandpa uses that I never understood until this moment.

But—I need to reenergize because we have a YouTube video to film!

As I approach the Make You Up doors, I text Elliot the code words: peppermint mocha. We invited Cheyenne to the filming as well, but she sent her regrets. She has a date with her mom to binge the most recent season of *The Bachelorette*. I felt the same tiny tug of annoyance as earlier—no, not annoyance—jealousy. I can't remember the last time we had an HGTV Greenberg family marathon, sprawled out with blankets and candy and mercilessly judging people for their design preferences. I always predict "flip," and my moms always predict "flop," and it's a whole cute thing.

Elliot cracks open the store door, pulling me out of my

thoughts. He peers both ways like we're in a heist movie and not a suburban mall that hasn't had a proper facelift since the early aughts. Then he nods and lets me in, whispering, "All clear."

"Copy," Geraldine's voice responds.

Elliot's phone sticks out of his pocket, functioning as a walkie-talkie on speakerphone. I lean over and speak into it. "The peppermint mocha has landed. Over."

"Copy," Geraldine responds again.

I grin. "This is fun."

Elliot grins back. "Very fun. Now get in here."

He locks the door behind us, and I follow him to the back of the store. It looks so different after hours, less impressive. Without the display lights and hordes of shoppers, the products don't have the same magical shine. And yet Geraldine trails around the rows of makeup with eyes glazed over like a kid in a candy store, or like a Geraldine in a makeup store. When she sees us, she squeals and runs over. "This is the coolest thing ever! And that includes the time Lucille Tifton's friend liked my tweet about Lucille Tifton. Thank you for this most brilliant idea, my most brilliant friends."

"It was all Shoshanna!" Elliot says.

"Nuh-uh," I reply. "I'm not taking all of the credit. I mean, yes, I will totally take some of the credit because I am indeed an awesome friend, but this wouldn't be possible without Elliot's brave risk-taking."

"It's for a worthy cause," he replies solemnly.

"Okay!" Geraldine claps her hands together. "I guess we should get started, then!" She flits around the store like an absolute pro, plucking mascara samples from one brand and concealer from another and lipstick from a third. Her fingers trail along the product options like they have a mind of their own. Once she has her artillery gathered, she organizes it all on the table for filming, while Elliot and I set up the backdrop from Once Upon. Then we even focus two of the store lights in Geraldine's direction so it looks totally professional.

"Ready to start?" I ask, holding up her phone, prepared to film.

"Yeah!" Geraldine replies, face bright under the lights, but then her smile falters.

"Hey." I put the phone down. "What's wrong?"

Her burgundy-lacquered nails tap against a mascara tube. "I guess I'm nervous?"

That might be a first for Geraldine Castillo. I might be impulsive, but Geraldine has always been the daring one. In elementary school, when everyone else was scared of the long monologue, she volunteered to be the lead in the play. In middle school, we went to Six Flags, and she marched right up to the most extreme roller coaster, while the rest of us tested the waters with the baby rides. And last year when we attended a protest for gun reform, a reporter asked if any high school students wanted to be interviewed, and she stepped right up to the microphone, her voice not wobbling once.

It's disarming to see Geraldine second-guess.

And it tells me how much this means to her.

"Don't be nervous!" Elliot says. "No one will even see this!"

Geraldine's face falls, and I elbow him in the side. "Way to be supportive, dude."

"Well, they *won't*," he says.

"Yeah." I pause. "I guess that's true." I walk over to Geraldine, put my hands on her shoulders, and stare into her beautiful brown eyes. "Geraldine, my best friend, you are smart and gorgeous and suspiciously good at liquid eyeliner, like obviously you made a deal with the devil to get a line that straight. This video is going to be a slam dunk, which is a sports thing that people say. And if somehow it's not a slam dunk, no one will see it anyway, which sounds rude when Elliot says it but actually is a great reason to not be nervous, okay?"

She gives a weak laugh. "Okay."

I pause, then inspect her face just to be sure and realize she has a little smudge on her cheek, maybe from her shift at Bo's. I lick my finger and wipe at it.

"Hey!" Geraldine shouts.

"What?" I ask. "You had some schmutz."

Now she's laughing hard. "Okay, *thanks, Mom*."

"You're welcome, sweetie." I return to filming position. "All right, beautiful. Let's do this!"

* * *

The filming goes great. I don't spot a hint of nerves on camera. It's still wild to me Geraldine was unsure of herself for even a second, because she's so freaking talented and personable. With her brilliant smile and soothing voice, she showcased a few makeup tricks, including how to apply lip liner without making it look like you're wearing lip liner. Witchcraft, basically. She should really post the video so people can take advantage of her tips.

"Thank you, again," Geraldine tells me as we walk to our cars. Elliot, who finds even a seventy-degree day chilly, sprinted to his mom's car the second she arrived to pick him up. They're idling in the parking lot now, making sure Geraldine and I get into our cars safely.

"You are more than welcome." I wrap my arm around her shoulder and kiss her cheek, already chilled from the cold. We lapse into a comfortable silence the way only old friends can, and suddenly I feel a huge rush of gratefulness that I have Geraldine in my life. "Love you," I say.

She glances at me, her eyes crinkling with warmth. "As much as mint chocolate chip ice cream on a hot summer day?"

I laugh, immediately flashing back to that day in fourth grade when Geraldine dropped her freshly scooped ice-cream cone on the ground. I'd saved my week's allowance for my mint chocolate chip sundae and had a spoon full of ice cream and fudge poised in front of my mouth when her waffle cone cracked to pieces. Without hesitation, I locked eyes with Geraldine and solemnly told her, "Get an extra spoon," and together we downed my sundae in under a minute, sticky faced and smiling.

"Absolutely," I reply now.

She winks at me as we get to my car, then waves goodbye. I climb into Barbra and put my key in the ignition. All I want to do is get home, change into pj's, and collapse into bed. But I think back to the tension this morning over an empty pantry and drag Barbra to the grocery store instead. It's the grimy one that's open late at night and always has products on the edge of expiration and at least two aisles with flickering fluorescent lights, like horror movie is the theme of the store or something. I walk down the rows of food with sore feet and fill the cart with bread and deli meat and eggs and Mom's favorite pistachio ice cream even though it's not on sale and that sugary-sweet orange marmalade Mama likes.

The cashier rings everything up to $27.42, and she kind of has to tug my debit card from my fingers. I'm sure my moms would pay me back for the groceries, but that means I'd have to tell them, and then they'd snipe at each other, and it would defeat the whole purpose. I'll just put the groceries on the shelves and hope they assume the other bought them. No one will be fighting when there's delicious marmalade and pistachio ice cream to be had.

When the cashier hands back the receipt, I stuff it into

my pocket and push the number out of my mind. With my savings, holiday hours, and the bonus, I'll still have enough to fix Barbra. Jake was messing with me earlier. There's no way he could actually sell more books than me. I carry the groceries back to my car and take a deep breath, determined. That bonus is mine.

I fall asleep the second I hit my mattress. Heavy sleep. Drool-on-the-mattress sleep. So when a door slams open in the middle of the night, I snap awake, disoriented in the dark. Muffled voices seep from the hallway into my room. Fighting voices.

My stomach clenches as the voices grow even louder.

"Stop being dramatic, Alex."

"It's called *caring*, Alana."

"You think I don't care? You think I work fifty hours a week and do everything around this house because I don't care?"

"Alana, you're—"

"I'm not having this conversation again—" The voices become too muffled to hear. My heart thrums against my chest, so hard I can feel its beat in my ears. I clutch my blanket closer to my body, scared for some reason they might storm into my room, like *I've* done something wrong.

Then Mama's voice appears again. "I'm going back to bed!"

"Fine!" Mom shouts.

Their bedroom door closes.

Silence.

I'm wide-awake now. Before I can think about why, I'm sliding out of bed and creeping over to my door. My pulse races as I crack it open. Mom is there, in the hallway, her feet shoved into her sheepskin loafers. She turns at the noise and startles when she sees me. It takes her a moment to adjust, almost like she forgot I lived here. She blinks twice. "Shoshanna." The skin under her eyes is dark, either from lack of sleep or rubbed eyeliner. "I'm sorry. We woke you?"

My throat feels scratchy as I take in her shoes and the sweater draped over her arm. "Where are you going?"

"Just . . . out to pick up milk."

"I got some," I say, blowing my cover. "I went to the grocery store."

"No, I think you forgot milk." Her eyes don't quite meet mine. "It wasn't in the fridge."

I forgot milk? "Oh," I say. "Sorry."

Mom pulls on her sweater and looks toward the staircase, away from me, as she says, "I'll be back soon."

"I could come with you. . . ." I offer despite the fact it's god knows what time in the middle of the night, I'm wearing pj's, and I have a full day of work tomorrow, but Mom's shaking her head before I finish the sentence. She doesn't want me with her, doesn't want to spend time with me. I can feel it, deep down in my knotted stomach.

"I'll be back soon," she repeats.

"Okay."

And then she's gone, and the house is once again quiet.

I stand there in the hallway for a long moment before returning to my room. Dread tightens around my spine. And my pulse is racing too fast, no chance of falling back asleep now. Who gets milk in the middle of the night? What were they fighting about? And why does it seem so much worse than before? In the dark, I slip under my covers and unlock my phone. My hands are shaking, and I close my eyes and take a breath. What if . . . what if things are worse than I thought? What if they get a . . .

My brain shuts down at the thought of that word.

No. It's not possible. The women who moved in together five months after meeting, the women who raised me in a warm cocoon of finger paints and oatmeal chocolate-chip cookies, the women who, without fail, go to their favorite restaurant for Thai food, split two bottles of prosecco, and call in "sick" to work the next day every year on their anniversary, those women do not get a divorce.

I swallow hard.

It feels like I'm rocking inside of a house that's perfectly still.

I just want to help. I want to fix it. But I don't know how. I start scrolling through my phone, trying to numb the thoughts with one-shot fanfiction and memes. My eyes grow heavy and my head drowsy as I eventually make it to my camera roll and watch the video we filmed with Geraldine earlier. It's so good. *She's* so good. I hate that she doesn't feel self-assured enough to post it. I want to load her up with a thousand pounds of confidence, want her to realize her incredible talent, want her to believe in herself as much as I do. But, the thing is, sometimes we need outside validation as well, validation outside of friends and family. Geraldine deserves all the validation in the world.

If I can't figure out how to help my moms, at least I can help my best friend. Before I know it, I'm signing up for a YouTube account and uploading her video. My brain buzzes with the potent mix of adrenaline and sleep deprivation. Once it's live, I copy the link to the video and tap from one beauty YouTuber to the next, commenting on how great their videos are even though I haven't watched them, and saying, "Hey! Have you checked out this new girl Geraldine? She's pretty great too!" I try my best to play six degrees of separation so it doesn't look like I'm spamming feeds.

After sending the video to a dozen people, my eyelids take control and dip closed, and I fall back asleep. But I don't sleep well. I toss and turn. I hear doors open and close. And then, when I do stay asleep, my dreams are scattered, tense, and as I drowsily roll over for the hundredth time, I remember something—

I did buy milk. A whole gallon of 2 percent.

Chapter Seven

I'm early for my shift, and Once Upon won't open for another fifteen minutes, but I couldn't stick around home this morning, waiting to see if fighting would erupt again. Something is broken. Cracked. And I don't know how to fix it.

Soft acoustic rock plays from the store speakers, and only half of the lights are on, but I can tell from her open door that Myra is already hard at work in her office. "Shoshanna!" Daniel's voice calls out to me as I step farther into the store. "Help us decorate the tree!"

I turn a corner to find Daniel wrapping a strand of twinkle lights around our artificial tree. I hesitate when I see Jake working next to him, blue-and-green flannel sleeves pushed up to his elbows, exposing his forearms as he positions the lights just so. *Really?* He's in early too? Home is so tense. I don't want to keep my defensives at Once Upon as well.

They finish with the string of lights and then sit on the

floor, surrounded by more lights and tins of popcorn. "Sit. Help." Daniel pats the floor. "Please?"

I rock back on my heels. "Yeah, I'm Jewish."

Daniel laughs. "I'm aware. And, hey, Jake is Jewish too."

So that's confirmed. I glance at Jake and his brown curls, while he untangles lights with impressive intensity. Jake Kaplan. Jewish boy. Attractive Jewish boy. Rude, attractive Jewish boy untangling lights for a Christmas tree.

Jake glances up at me with a half smile. "Maybe we can find a Star of David to put on top."

I waver. His smile seems genuine, and it'd be nice to sit with my work husband and a bunch of shiny baubles and lights before the store opens. I could use the peace, the comfort and calm. I twist my necklace once before relenting with an "Okay." The back of my neck heats as I sit down next to Jake, acutely aware his knee is a mere inch from mine. I could scoot over, make more room, but Jake might laugh— and also, I don't want to scoot away from his knee.

Instead, I grab a tin of popcorn and string. I stare at the items and then up at Daniel. "Um, yeah, I have no idea what to do with these."

"It would be weird if you did." Daniel grins and then grabs the popcorn and passes me some knotted lights instead. "My grandma had me stringing popcorn when I was seven, so now I'm a board-certified expert with over a decade of experience. Can you untangle lights?"

"I can certainly try!" I reply.

I focus on the lights, and for a few minutes, we all work in comfortable silence. An acoustic version of a Beatles song comes on, and I hum along, grateful for the break from Christmas music. I even notice Jake tapping a foot next to me as I pull out one knot after another. The task is nice, satisfying, and tension eases from my shoulders.

"Blech! Gross!" Daniel coughs into his hand.

My eyes go from him to the tin of popcorn. "Did you just eat that?" I ask.

"I don't think you're supposed to eat the popcorn," Jake says. And then he catches my eye, and there's this spark as we both laugh, and my stomach swoops with the pleasure of it. Jake's laugh is like snow in Georgia, so rare you can't help but stop and pay attention to it.

I look back at Daniel with warm cheeks.

"I was hungry." He shrugs. "I'm a growing boy."

"Tell you what," Jake says. "I have a killer salted caramel popcorn recipe. I'll bring some in for y'all."

For y'all. Jake Kaplan is going to bring *me* popcorn? And he says *y'all*? Oh geez. The stomach swooping intensifies because apparently my body hasn't picked up on the message that we don't like this particular Southern Jewish boy. I keep my eyes on Daniel and ask, "Where's the popcorn from?"

"Myra gave it to me." He scratches the back of his head. "A week ago. And then I forgot to decorate the tree, which is why we're all doing it this morning so, you know, she doesn't fire me."

"Please," I say. "Myra would never fire you. And she definitely wouldn't fire you during the holidays."

"Maybe you're right. We're too busy to lose staff right now."

I glance around. Since the store isn't open yet, it's still empty in here, but soon a rush of customers will fill the aisles. "Definitely," I say. "Especially after a quiet year."

"Yeah, it has been empty lately." Daniel shakes his fist. "Damn you, online retailers."

I snort. "You were just talking about how much you love the Avengers shirt you ordered online."

"So, I'm a Marvel-loving hypocrite, whatever."

"Mm-hmm," I say, now concentrated back on my lights. I'm faced with a particularly difficult knot and can't seem to get a grip on it. My fingers feel as graceful as meat cleavers. "Grr."

"Here, give it." I glance up to find Jake looking at me. His eyes are soft and a bit amused, and this time my stomach doesn't swoop—it freaking flutters. Jewish god damn it. I shrug and pass him the lights, ignoring the tingle I feel when our fingers brush together. In three deft pulls, Jake has the lights untangled. His self-satisfied smile is both attractive and annoying. The duality of man. "You're welcome," he says, passing the lights back to me.

"Thanks." I force a grin. "Nice to know you're good at something."

"Oh, I'm good at a lot of things," Jake replies. The look he then gives me should be R-rated for mature audiences only. My skin flushes, and I swallow hard as he picks up another knotted string and untangles it with his dexterous fingers in seconds.

"Guys . . . ," Daniel says. "C'mon. Play nice."

"We are playing nice!" My voice comes out both an octave and a decibel too high. "I was complimenting him on being good at something, since, you know, he's not very good at selling books."

"Wouldn't be so certain about winning that bonus if I were you," Jake says.

I narrow my eyes. "Is that a threat?"

He shrugs, totally cool and calm. "Maybe."

"*Maybe.* What does that mean?"

"You'll find out later today."

"Like you could really—"

Suddenly the soft acoustic music shuts off and is replaced by "Rudolph the Red Nosed Reindeer" blasting at top volume. The blaring jingle disarms me, and I lose focus on what I was about to say.

"Oh, look! We're open!" Daniel comments. He mutters the next part under his breath. "Just in time."

* * *

Three hours of bookselling later, I walk into the break room, ready to scarf down my turkey sandwich and chips. I nod at Tanya, who smiles and gives a small wave, charm bracelet jingling on her wrist, before she returns her eyes to her book. My lunchtime doesn't line up with my friends today, and anyway, I want to avoid the food court and temptation of spending money. I packed my lunch with tense muscles this morning, wincing at the loud crinkle of the chip packaging, trying not to wake up Mom and Mama.

I sit down and pull a book out of my tote bag. It's historical fiction about a vigilante, murdering doctress in the nineteenth century. It's excellent, but I've been so busy with the holiday season, I've barely had time to read it. As I search for my bookmark, which always seems to slip between the pages like we're playing a game of hide-and-seek, my phone buzzes. Hmm, probably just spam, but no—it's an e-mail from YouTube, and suddenly I remember I posted Geraldine's video online last night. My heart pounds as I bring up the page and gasp. Literally *gasp*. Like Tanya looks over at me from her own book and lunch of tuna fish and crackers and says, "Everything all right, dear?" *Gasp*.

"Yes!" I reply, excitement flooding through me. "All good!"

My eyes widen as I take in the number: 923. Almost a *thousand* people have viewed Geraldine's video. *A thousand!* In just one night! And there are comments as well, thanking her for all of the cool tips. Oh my god. I knew it. People love

Geraldine. I have to tell her! But it would be awesome if we could crack a thousand views first.

I send links to a few more YouTubers, including, after racking my brain for the name, that Lucille Tifton girl that Geraldine is obsessed with. She probably won't watch the video, but hopefully other people in her thousands of comments will be curious and click the link. I can't believe this worked!

As I'm finishing up, my phone buzzes with a text message from Mama: Thanks for the marmalade, darling.

My chest hums with contentment. Maybe my cover was blown about the groceries, but it was better than leaving the pantry empty. And maybe I can do something more to help, something more than washing dishes and buying groceries. *Maybe I can . . . Oh, that would be perfect . . .*

"Yes!" I shout for a second time. Tanya looks up again. I give her an apologetic smile. "All good, promise. Want some chips?"

"No thanks, sweetie," she replies with a smile, turning back to her book yet again.

And I am *all good*. I text my moms and ask them to be home in time for dinner tonight. I tell them I'm cooking us pasta. But I'm not cooking us pasta. I'm going to get them Thai from their favorite restaurant, and they'll actually sit down and talk and listen and remember why they love each other so freaking much in the first place. Ooh! What if I could get prosecco as well, so it could be just like one of their anniversary dinners? Hmm, the Thai food alone will push my budget for Barbra to the limit . . . though maybe . . .

"Hey, Tanya," I say, interrupting her again. She puts her book down on the table this time and looks at me with the patience of a saint. I twirl a piece of my hair and smile wide. "Can you do me a favor? Pretty please?"

Tanya agrees to buy two bottles of prosecco in exchange for three free babysitting sessions for her boys next year and a promise I'll snap a photo of my moms with the alcohol— otherwise she'll storm my house to tell them I've been under-age drinking. It's kind of funny how easy it is to get alcohol when no one suspects you'd actually drink it. I also call the Thai restaurant and place my moms' staple order for delivery: shrimp pad thai, vegetable basil rice, and tom kha gai soup. The price isn't too bad—$37.24. With the wine-for-babysitting exchange and the bonus money, I'll still have enough for Barbra. Just enough. Like I might be couch diving for gas change the rest of the year.

Now if only my moms would actually text me back. I bite my nail as I leave the break room and check my phone one last time. No messages yet.

I wander down the young adult fiction aisle and am soon swept back up in the tide of bookselling. After helping half a dozen shoppers and sending them off to the registers with my QR code, I spot Jake and a customer in the nonfiction section. The woman smiles down at a tablet in her hands as Jake chats with her, nodding at something in agreement. What did he mean earlier about me not winning the bonus? What's the magic trick up his flannel sleeve?

I walk up to him and the customer, and in a breezy voice say, "Hello, I'm Shoshanna! Can I also assist you today?"

"Sure!" The woman smiles at me before glancing back at the tablet in her hands. "I'm just finishing up your quiz. This is awesome!"

"Our quiz?" I ask, leaning over to glance at the screen. It's some kind of Buzzfeed-style quiz, like the ones that sort you into your Harry Potter house and are always wrong, and how dare anyone say I'm anything other than a Ravenclaw?

The questions are straightforward yes-or-no.

Did you read this book? Yes.

Did you read this book? No.

Each answer generates a new, more niche title.

The woman is totally engrossed. I glance at Jake, who seems pleased as heck with himself, thumbs tucked into the pockets of his jeans. We both step back as the woman continues with the quiz. Jake leans toward me, his voice low enough to make my skin buzz. "Pretty cool, huh?" he asks.

"Um, I guess." I shrug. Seriously? *This* was his genius idea. No way some Buzzfeed quiz is going to outsell me. "Where'd you find it?"

"Oh, I didn't find it anywhere." Jake yawns, stretching one arm behind his back and tugging it with the other, exposing a sliver of his abdomen, like when I first met him only a couple days ago. He must do it on purpose. Sliver-of-skin-exposing, flannel-wearing mastermind. "Sorry." He grins at me. "Tired. It was a late night. I was up building that quiz."

"You . . ." I pause, feeling a tiny seed of panic. "You what?"

"I built the quiz," he repeats in a casual tone. "It's based off of Once Upon stock and weighted toward store bestsellers and staff recommendations."

"Oh!" the woman exclaims, looking up from the screen in delight. "Perfect! I had this on my list last year and forgot about it!"

"Perfect!" Jake smiles at her, then at me. I hate his white teeth. *Like, big deal you have good oral hygiene. Mazel tov, you floss. Show-off.* "I'll take you right to it."

Before they head off down the aisle, Jake passes the tablet to me. "Here, take a look if you want. Let me just . . ." He signs me into his *password-protected* quiz. His ridiculous popcorn-stringing, light-untangling dexterous fingers move too fast for me to even see the username, much less the password. He then leads the woman off as I look down at the screen. The design is attractive and clean. The quiz title asks: "What Is Your Next Great Read?"

I roll my eyes and push back the seed of panic. Please.

Like anything Jake builds could predict something I'd want to read. I sigh and start tapping answers. I'm led down the *Time Stands Still* category, but I mean, that's a major book. Like half the planet owns a copy, so of course it's on here. There's no way Jake can predict what I want to read next. Even I have trouble. . . .

"Damn it," I mutter.

The quiz leads me right to a fantasy series the author of *Time Stands Still* often recommends. I've been meaning to read it and keep forgetting. But still. That's pretty obvious. We print out recommendations like that on our receipts: "Do you read X? Then you might also like Y."

I'm sure if I picked more difficult options it wouldn't work . . . though, the book it selected for that woman has been out for years. And it's the author's only novel, so it's not a basic "other titles by this author" recommendation.

My shoulders tense as Jake rounds a corner. He walks back to me with so much confidence, with a grin so cocky, I want to kick out my foot and trip him. He takes the tablet back with one hand and runs fingers through his hair with the other. "Pretty cool, huh?" he asks. "Oh, wait. One second." Suddenly he pulls out a walkie-talkie. My eyes widen in shock as he presses the button, and the system buzzes overhead. "Jake to stockroom, we're low on Christmas Cat calendars again; Jake to stockroom, low on Christmas Cat calendars."

My voice is loud enough without a radio. "Myra gave you PA privileges? *Already?* You only started working here forty-eight hours ago!"

"Actually, forty-six." Jake winks. "To be exact."

My eyes narrow as I look back down at the tablet. "You don't read books. How did you make this quiz?"

"I read books," Jake responds, his tone short. A sick feeling courses through me. I didn't mean to say that again. It just slipped out and sounded all judgmental. "I read books for school. And Daniel's been giving me some stuff to read, and I—you know what? I don't need to explain myself to you."

"You're right," I say stiffly. "You don't. I'm sorry."

Silence stretches, the air crackling between us for a long moment, before Jake continues, "This doesn't have to do with reading, anyway. It's mostly coding and algorithms."

"But if you're so great with computers, why work here?" I ask genuinely. "Why not work at the Genius Bar?"

He steps closer to me, and I make the mistake of stepping closer too, and then I make the double mistake of inhaling, and he smells like chocolate cake and buttercream frosting, and I'm pretty much convinced this guy sleeps in a bakery every night, like is-there-a-Pillsbury-factory-nearby-and-does-Jake-have-a-bed-there convinced. "Because," he says, my pulse skipping as his dark eyes lock with mine, "here I get the satisfaction of besting you in this competition.

Might want to check the scoreboard, Shoshanna. Your lead is slipping."

My heart thumps, then races. He's lying. He has to be lying. There's no way he's beating me.

But the problem is, Jake doesn't *look* like he's lying.

"This—this is cheating!"

He rolls his eyes. "How is this cheating?"

"It's—I—" I spin around. "I'm going to Myra. Myra!"

And then I'm speed-walking toward Myra's office, and Jake is speed-walking behind me, muttering, "This is ridiculous! Why am I chasing you?"

And I'm saying, "You're right. Maybe you should stop!"

But he keeps going, and then we're both in the doorframe of Myra's office, panting a little, which really tells me I should speed-walk through the mall more often. Myra glances up from a giant stack of papers and gives me *the look*. Then she gives Jake *the look*. Then she pauses Frank Sinatra crooning from her speakers and asks, "This conversation is going to aggravate me, isn't it?"

"It had better!" I respond. "Jake is *cheating*."

"I am not cheating! I am—" He pauses, realizing he was shouting and looking embarrassed. Who's juvenile now, Jake? It takes every ounce of willpower to not stick my tongue out at him. "I am not cheating," he repeats, voice calm, but a hand clenched at his side. "I promise."

Myra nods. "I believe you, but could you do me a favor

and tell me why Shoshanna here *thinks* you're cheating?"

"I'll show you." Jake steps up to her desk. My stomach lurches as he shows her the quiz. I'm quickly regretting the second cup of sugar-laden coffee I drank earlier.

Myra says the good kind of "mmm" not the bad kind. "This is really something, Jake. You did this all on your own?"

"I have a friend who codes," he answers. "And Daniel helped."

"Daniel *what*?" I gasp. "Betrayer, first of his name."

"How are the customers responding?" Myra asks, ignoring me.

"Some don't want to take the quiz, but the ones who take it usually buy the recommended book."

"Great, love it. Keep it up." Myra glances at me next. "It's definitely not cheating, Shoshanna. Come on now. The store is packed. You need to be selling books, not distracting Jake from doing exactly that."

My throat gets all tight, and my face flushes, like I might start crying, which is a completely unreasonable response to my boss asking me to do my job. Myra is awesome, actually the best, and letting her down is not my favorite feeling. I take a quick breath. The last twelve hours have been a lot. I need a moment alone to recalibrate. Hoping my voice will be steady, I say, "I'm sorry. You're right."

"Good, thank you."

I hurry out of her office, and with no more eyes on me,

a few tears release, warm and wet against my cheeks. I wipe them away as I head through the break room and then into the stockroom, where I close the door behind me and slide down to the floor, wrapping my arms around my knees and trying to breathe and keep from breaking into full-fledged crying.

It's okay. Everything is going to be okay. I'm going to win the bonus. My moms are going to love their Thai dinner. And everything will return to the way it's always been.

"Why are you on the floor?" a voice asks.

Startled, I look up and find Arjun and Sophie-Anne on the other side of the storage room, unloading boxes. I quickly wipe at my face. "Nothing, no reason. Uh, I'm just tired. Dead tired."

"Zombie or vampire?" Sophie-Anne asks. She flips open one of the books and looks at the text on the flap.

"What?" I ask.

"Zombie or vampire?" Sophie-Anne repeats, slapping the book closed.

Arjun's silver chains jangle as he walks over to a box and slices it open. He explains, "You said you're dead. I think she wants to know what kind of dead you are—zombie or vampire?"

"Oh, right," I say, like that makes sense.

Sophie-Anne walks toward me. She leans over, blue eyes wide, blond hair falling in tendrils around her face. I blink

hard, for a second feeling like I'm staring up at Mama. Then she speaks. "Zombies have more physical strength, but vampires have more control. What do you want when you're eating people?" Her eyes widen. "Chaos or control?"

I scoot back against the door, mostly amused but with a healthy dose of fear. "Um, neither. Thank you for explaining, though."

"No problem!" Sophie-Anne replies.

"Ow," Arjun says in a monotone. I glance over. He has a paper cut on his index finger and is staring at the drop of blood.

"Ouch." I wince.

"Ooh!" Sophie-Anne wanders toward him.

"Please don't—" I say, but it's too late. "—lick the blood."

Sophie-Anne cleans off the finger with one swipe of her tongue.

"Oh my god," I groan.

"Thanks." Arjun gives her a dazed smile and then kisses her right on the lips.

"Y'all are disgusting."

"Aw!" Sophie-Anne squeals. "Thank you!"

My phone buzzes. It's a text from Myra asking me to come back to her office. Nerves stiffen my shoulders. Am I in trouble? What if she bans me from the competition? At least Arjun and Sophie-Anne were weird enough to stop my urge to cry again. I take a deep breath, then force myself up off the floor. "I'll see you guys later—" Sophie-Anne is now straddling Arjun on a box of books, fingers threaded through his hair. "And you're making out. Okay. Bye."

I really wish I could say this is the first time that's happened.

Chapter Eight

Myra's door is still open. Anxiety pulses through me, and I try to steady my thoughts. She's not going to kick me out of the competition. It's fine. Everything is fine, like in *The Good Place*. Wait, no. That's a terrible example.

I shake my head, then step into her office. Myra looks up at me and slides down her reading glasses. A pink crochet chain holds them like a necklace across her collar. "Hello, Shoshanna," she says, voice disconcertingly neutral.

"Hi." I lift my hand to bite at a nail, then embarrassed by the urge, lower it back down and stuff it into my pocket. "I'm sorry about earlier."

"Apology accepted," Myra replies. *"If."* She lets that "if" hang in the air an extra-long time. "You prove it. By working together with Jake."

At that exact moment, Jake pops into the office. My shoulders stiffen at the sight of him, and I feel a weird burst of irritation when he doesn't even look at me. "You asked to see me?" he asks Myra.

"Yes." Myra glances between the two of us. "We have the event tomorrow with Liv Childers."

Oh! Of course we do. With everything going on, I almost forgot about the event even though it's been in the planning for months. Liv is the author of *Christmas Killings*. It's always awesome to have a great writer in the store, especially a kick-ass woman.

"Thanks to the scheduling gods hating me," Myra says, "you two are the only ones available for the early morning shift. I need you both here, bright and early, for setup. The rest of the staff will be in later to help as the event gets started."

Early morning setup. Alone with Jake. Not even with Daniel as a buffer. My palms suddenly feel clammy.

"*But*," Myra continues, leaning forward in her chair, "because it will take all morning, you can give the customers your QR codes when you check them out for the signing, and it'll count toward your numbers for the competition, all right?"

My attitude brightens. *Now that's a silver lining.* "Really?" I ask. "There'll be, like, hundreds of people here!"

"Really." Myra nods.

"Thank you!" I say.

"Awesome, thank you," Jake agrees.

"You're welcome." Her tone grows serious again as her eyes cut from Jake to me. "But split the sales in half evenly. No arguing and squabbling. I'll ban you both from the competition if it happens again. I'm serious. Do you understand?"

"Yes," Jake says. He does glance at me this time, and I swear his expression screams, *If she won't, I won't.*

"Got it," I reply. "Promise."

"Good. Now take these extra codes."

Jake grabs his codes and leaves, but I stay behind, twisting my fingers together. These sales tomorrow will ensure my lead over most of my coworkers, but if his quiz works, Jake might be right at the top with me. As much as I don't want to admit it, there's a chance he could win this competition, and I'll have to earn the money to fix Barbra next year.

"What's up?" Myra asks, pulling back on her glasses as her eyes focus on her computer. Maybe she's working on her next book. She writes mystery novels and signed with a literary agent last year because, you know, she's awesome.

"Um," I say. "I was wondering if I could get more hours after the New Year. I was only working a couple days a week last semester, and three or four days would be better. I'm trying to—"

"Sorry, no can do," Myra cuts me off.

"Oh," I say. "Well maybe—"

"We have too much staff as it is. Great for the holidays, but everyone is going to be fighting for extra hours again soon." Myra lifts her eyes to mine. "In fact, we might need to cut hours. The store is slow most of the year, so we only need a couple of people here at a time. If you need additional hours, I suggest looking elsewhere."

Elsewhere. She means look elsewhere for *extra* hours, right?

Or—what if she means I should leave Once Upon altogether?

"Anything else?" Myra asks.

"Uh, no. Thank you."

"Sure thing." She turns back to her computer.

I leave her office and tug on my necklace, twisting the chain around my finger, tighter and tighter.

Tanya dropped the bottles of prosecco off in a cooler outside the front door, and the Thai food will be delivered to our house in an hour, but my moms still haven't responded to my text, which means they won't be home to drink the prosecco and meet the deliveryman, much less to have a healing dinner full of love and reminiscing. A headache blooms near my temple as I check my messages yet again, wondering if I somehow missed a text, knowing I didn't.

It's weird.

For my entire life, my moms have always texted me back. It seems like an inconsequential thing, texting, yet knowing they'll respond has always been a constant. But now my phone is silent. And my stomach seems to have tied itself into a pretzel more knotted than the ones at Auntie Anne's.

"C'mon," I mutter, staring at my phone, like I can magic it into buzzing. That anti-Semite Roald Dahl set me up to believe we could all have magical powers like Matilda. Jerk, for so many reasons.

Why won't my moms respond? Are they busy? Is pasta dinner with their daughter not enticing enough? Do they just not care? *Come on. Buzz. Buzz!* "Darn it!" I scream, tossing my phone on the table. It lands with a hard *thwack*. I yelp and immediately scoop it back up, panicked I broke it.

The screen is fine, but still no messages. "Screw it," I mutter, then type out a text to both of them: Hey moms, had a really hard day at work. Not doing well and need to see you both. Please come home for dinner. Okay? It's an emergency!

I send off the text, shove my phone in my pocket, and hope for the best as I finish up my shift.

"Shoshanna." Arjun calls my name in a monotone over the loudspeaker just as I'm about to leave for the evening. "Your mom is on line one."

At first, I laugh because it sounds like a bad *your mom* joke. But then my muscles tense. Why is Mom calling at work? I rush over to the registers and grab the phone from Arjun, mouthing *Thank you* while he gives me a slow blink in response. I worry about that kid. "Hey, Mom," I breathe into the phone. "Everything okay?"

"So you are there," she says.

I loop the phone cord around my finger. My generation really is missing out on phone-cord fidgeting. "Yeah. Is everything—"

"And you're not hurt?" she cuts me off, her tone curt. "And you're okay?"

"Yeah, I'm fine. Did you—"

"Shoshanna." My muscles clench as she snaps out my name. "Let me get this straight. You told us there's an *emergency*, but you're at work and completely fine? Nothing is wrong?" Her tone is so severe that it makes the floor sway beneath me.

I finally manage to reply in a meek whisper, "Nothing is wrong."

At least, not in the way she means.

"Come straight home from work," she commands. "We'll talk then."

The line clicks off, and I shut my eyes tight. The ground keeps swaying. *Breathe, Shoshanna. Breathe.*

"Are you okay?" a voice asks.

My eyes pop open, and I realize it's Arjun. *Arjun* is asking if I'm okay. That can't be a good sign. I nod my head. "Yeah, fine. Thanks."

"Okay." He shrugs and goes back to work.

I grab my things from the break room and rush out of the store and into the mall, shoving past the chaos of customers, knocking into shoulders and bags and many, many strollers. My heart pounds in my ears as I make a beeline for the Gap, where I know Cheyenne is finishing up her shift as well. I enter the store and push past more shoppers and racks of sweaters and cut through a zigzagging line for the register, dizzily asking someone where Cheyenne is, and they point me to the break room, which looks almost identical to our break room, and when I find Cheyenne sitting at a table with Geraldine, relief swoops through me. Thank goodness they're both here. "Guys," I say, my voice constricted. "I think my moms, well, it's just, I haven't—"

As I try to figure out the right words, I realize my friends aren't looking at me with concern or interest—they're looking at me in annoyance, anger even.

Anxiety squeezes like a vice around my spine.

"Um," I say. "What's going on?"

Geraldine blinks, her eyes watering. Her lips part to say something but then close again, so Cheyenne speaks for her. She pushes up the sleeves of her forest-green sweater and stares me right in the eyes. "Shoshanna, you posted Geraldine's video online without permission. Seriously? Who does that?"

Oh. Tension clogs my throat. "I'm sorry," I say, stepping forward. "I guess—I shouldn't have done that. I'm sorry, Geraldine, but I just wanted to show you how talented you are! And you got so many views—almost a thousand! Actually, I bet more than a thousand, now. Let me just—"

"It's a lot more than a thousand." Geraldine finally speaks, her voice eerily calm as her fingers tighten into a death grip around her phone. "Try fourteen thousand."

Wait. What? My brain whirs, trying to make sense of that number. But a number that large makes no sense at all.

Cheyenne helps again. She wraps a protective arm around Geraldine's shoulder, while looking straight at me. "It was a practice video, Shoshanna. No one was supposed to see it. Geraldine was just getting comfortable on camera, so she didn't need to come up with original content. She used ideas from a beauty influencer. From *Lucille Tifton*."

"Lucille Tifton," I say, the words hollow in my dry mouth.

"Yup," Cheyenne responds. "And then *someone* tagged Lucille in the video, and her fans discovered the stolen content, alerted her, and now Lucille and all her minions are slamming Geraldine online."

My head swims with panic, and my pulse races so fast I wonder if I'll pass out in the Gap and what type of business liability insurance they have. "I'm sorry," I say. "I'm so sorry, but how could I have known that—"

"You couldn't have known," Geraldine cuts me off. Tears run down her cheeks, but her eyeliner and mascara are still in devastatingly perfect condition. "But you didn't need to know. Because the video was mine—mine to post. Not yours. You need to think, Shoshanna."

"I'm sorry," I whisper.

"I don't care," she shoots back.

"Please, let me fix—"

"Just go, Shoshanna," Cheyenne says. Her hard gaze drops a pit in my stomach. "Just leave us alone."

There are worried text messages from my moms, then angry ones. I don't see them until I climb into Barbra, my hands shaking both from my nerves and the freezing cold. As I scroll through them, my stomach churns so hard I can almost feel bile in my throat.

Honey, where are you?

Are you okay?

What's wrong? You said emergency.

We're worried. You aren't picking up.

Pick up your phone.

We're calling the store.

You're at work? And you're fine?

Come home immediately.

Don't you dare say emergency ever again if you're okay.

I put my phone on the passenger seat.

"Okay" is a very relative term.

When I walk into the house, there's a distinct called-to-the-principal's-office vibe. Mom and Mama are sitting in the living room, actually together on the same couch, holding a glass of prosecco each, but their faces are both stern.

Bubbles have never looked more depressing.

"Oh, good," Mom says, voice clipped with sarcasm. "You're in one piece."

Mama puts a hand on her knee, then takes it away just as quickly. "No need to take everything to a ten, Alana," she mutters.

"She said it was an *emergency*," Mom cuts back. "She's

sixteen and acting six with this classic girl-who-cried-wolf nonsense."

"*Enough*," Mama says to her. She glances at me next and offers a wavering smile. "C'mon, darling. Sit down."

I clear my throat and sit on a chair closest to her. Mama's blond hair falls in waves around her shoulders. It's smooth and shiny like someone in the pages of a magazine. Mom gave birth to me, so Mama's straight hair is the blond sheep of the family. I love my curls, but sometimes I'm jealous of the smoothness and ease of Mama's hair. Sometimes everything about me feels too complicated.

My dress is wrinkled from a day of work. I try to smooth it out, then find a loose thread at the hem. The sight irritates me, but if I yank the thread, the whole dress might unravel.

"Shoshanna," Mom says. I yank out the thread, quick, then snap my attention back to my parents. It's disarming, having Mom's full attention, something I haven't felt for a while now. Her eyes bore into me, and my skin feels too tight. I dig a finger into my leggings. "Why did you say there was an emergency?" she asks.

"And why did you buy us Thai food?" Mama adds. "We want you to save your money for Ms. Streisand."

"I, well . . ." I swallow hard, hating the wobble in my voice as I speak. "You guys have been fighting a lot. And you even missed Latkepalooza. And I wanted to help make things okay again, so I washed dishes and brought groceries, but that didn't fix anything. . . . I thought maybe if you had time alone together that would help. And you always celebrate your anniversary with Thai food, so I got Thai food and tried to get you both home at the same time."

Mama laughs, light and amused. "Darling, did you try to *Parent Trap* us?"

My cheeks burn. "Maybe a little."

"Well, you can't," Mom says. "We aren't characters in a movie, or in some book you're writing. We're people, and you can't force people to—"

"*Alana*," Mama warns yet again.

Mom pauses, and when she continues, her voice comes out softer. "Shoshanna, we love you." Her eyes connect with mine, and I see the love right there in them. I swallow hard and glance away. "We love you so much. But pretending there's an emergency when there's not one is unacceptable behavior. We were *worried* about you. I—" Her voice cracks. "I was very worried about you."

Mama grabs Mom's hand and squeezes it.

"I'm sorry," I whisper, mouth dry. Mom sighs, but her voice stays soft. "I know you're sorry, but you're too old to act like this, Shoshanna. You need to grow up."

"It's late," Mama says. "Everyone is tired. Why don't we discuss this more tomorrow? All right?"

"All right," Mom agrees.

I nod and twist my hands together. "All right."

I head up to my room, thoughts clouded, dense. The thing is, I know it's wrong to pretend there's an emergency when there isn't one. I shouldn't have done that. But did I really cry wolf? Can my parents really tell me everything is okay when I know, without a doubt, it's not?

Chapter Nine

No, no, no," I whisper, my pulse racing as I again turn my key in the ignition. "Don't do this to me, Barbra. Do not do this to me. Not today." The engine grinds and grinds but refuses to start. *"Damn it."* My voice cracks.

I will myself not to cry because crying would be ridiculous, and also I can't spare the water because I don't hydrate enough, even though Cheyenne is always reminding me to drink more water . . . *Cheyenne. Geraldine.* My friends are so mad at me. They haven't responded at all to my litany of apology texts.

I fall back against my cold seat with a giant exhale. It's freezing outside, wind rattling bare branches, the sun muted behind dense gray clouds. I check my phone with frozen fingers. It's seven in the morning. My moms are still asleep, and my entire body tenses at the thought of waking them up to ask for a ride. Especially Mom.

I used to go to her for help with everything, but I feel like anything I ask her now will be met with a hard stare, with exasperation or disappointment.

I can't believe last night blew up in my face like that.

I can't believe I thought it *wouldn't* blow up in my face like that.

You need to think, Geraldine told me.

You need to grow up, Mom told me.

I also need to find a ride to work.

If I don't leave soon, I'll be late, which is the opposite of a grown-up thing to do, especially when this event is so important. And on top of that, if I'm late Myra might ban me from the bookselling competition, and then I won't have the money to fix Barbra, and then this will be a problem every morning, and—

I can see my frosted breath in front of me, quick, hard exhales. My pulse races as tears slip out of my eyes and down my cheeks. *Stop it, Shoshanna.* I'm overreacting. I'm being too sensitive. I'm crying, like a little kid. If I could just be a normal person for like ten seconds, I could calm down and figure out a solution. I know there must be one. Someone must be able to give me a ride. But no one in their right mind is awake at this hour on a holiday break. Not a single—

Oh.

Well. There is one person definitely awake right now.

"Ugh," I mutter, but unlock my phone before I can change my mind. My numb fingers search through my inbox for the latest Once Upon e-mail with a schedule and employee names and contact info. I find the number I need, tap it, and then press the phone to my ear. One ring, two rings. *Don't pick up. Just don't—*

"Hello?"

My heart jumps.

"Hello?" the voice asks again. It's low, gravelly, like he just rolled out of his warm bed.

"Hey, Jake." I clear my throat. "It's Shoshanna."

An old Toyota Camry pulls alongside the front of my driveway. The passenger window rolls down, and I find it's Jake in that seat, his hair rumpled like he really did just roll out of his warm bed. A warm feeling blooms in my stomach as he gives me a slight nod before returning to the spiral notebook in his lap and scribbling something down. With much more enthusiasm, a woman leans over him, seat belt straining so she can see me from the driver's side. "Hi, Shoshanna!" she says. "I'm Jake's mom! It's so nice to meet one of his coworkers. Hop on in!"

Jake's mom. I'm meeting Jake Kaplan's mom.

Oh my god.

I grab my tote bag and slide into the backseat. It's warm in here, and I bite back a groan of relief as my body defrosts. Mrs. Kaplan turns to me with a bright smile. "Morning!" she chirps.

"Morning!" I reply.

Mrs. Kaplan has short curly hair and lipstick the color of fresh strawberries. My smile falters when I think of how Geraldine would immediately ask for the name of that color. I click in my seat belt as Mrs. Kaplan turns back to Jake with a tsk. "You have some schmutz, Jakey," she tells him, before licking her finger and wiping his cheek.

Schmutz. Jakey. Finger spit cheek wipe. Amazing.

"Thanks, Mom," Jake says. He doesn't seem the least bit embarrassed, which is actually quite endearing. *Oy vey. Do I find Jake Kaplan endearing?*

"And thank *you* for the ride, Mrs. Kaplan," I say, trying to draw my focus back to her. "It's nice to meet you!"

"Just Ms. Kaplan," she replies, checking her mirrors before pulling away from the curb. Her car is old, not a relic like Barbra, but the seats are worn in well, and there's a radio instead of a Siri Bluetooth Wireless Robots Take Over the World set-up. As we drive, she tells Jake to "Pass me some almonds, tatala."

I glow at the word "tatala." It's nice to hear someone other than my moms—and Myra—speak Yiddish. It's nice to feel connected, even if it's to Jake Kaplan.

"Sure," Jake replies. As he leans forward to pull a bag from the glove box, my eyes flick across the back of his neck and the small patch of skin exposed between his hair and shirt collar. I bite the inside of my cheek and busy myself with organizing the contents of my tote: a book, tampons, a crushed granola bar, chamomile tea for Tanya, a scarf, another book . . .

"Want some almonds, Shoshanna?" Ms. Kaplan asks. "Jake seasons them himself. Oh, they're so tasty! My favorite addiction."

"*Mom*," Jake says.

"What? I can't be proud of your talent?"

"They're just almonds," he answers, but I can sense the smile in his voice.

Ms. Kaplan's overt pride pinches my stomach. In eighth grade, we wrote a short essay every week for my English class. My moms loved my essays so much they'd have me read them aloud in the living room. They'd literally applaud afterward. Sometimes even whistle. It was embarrassing. But also it was sweet, and I kind of really miss it. I haven't shared any writing with them lately. Not that I've been writing much at all lately.

"Here, try some," Ms. Kaplan says, passing me the bag.

"You really don't have to," Jake adds.

"No." I take the bag. "I want to."

I pop an almond into my mouth and *whoa*.

Like. Whoa.

The almond is smoked and peppery and salty and just freaking delicious.

"What kind of almond wizardry is this?" I ask.

"Told you!" Ms. Kaplan laughs. I grab a handful before passing the bag back up front.

"It's nothing," Jake says.

"He's a genius," Ms. Kaplan announces.

I nosh on the almonds and settle deeper into the backseat. The warm air blasting from the vents turns the car into a cozy cocoon, the Temptations play from the radio, and Ms. Kaplan talks and talks with Jake and me occasionally chiming in. It's nice, starting the day this way, with cheer and chatter, and before I know it, we're pulling into the mall parking lot. "Thank you again for driving me," I tell Ms. Kaplan. "I really appreciate it."

"Such lovely manners!" She beams. "Jake, doesn't she have lovely manners?"

Jake coughs. I resist the urge to kick the back of his seat.

Ms. Kaplan continues, "Jakey told me about the event at your store today. I love Liv Childers. Wish I could be there!"

"I'm sure Jake can get you a signed copy!" I suggest.

"Would you, tatala?" she asks.

"It's only in hardback, Mom."

"Oh, well that's okay, then," she replies.

"Totally get it." I nod. "I'm a paperback reader too. I love breaking the spine."

There's an uncomfortable silence after I say that. My shoulders tense. Usually I know the exact moment I put my foot in my mouth, but this time I'm not sure what I said wrong. *Darn it. Can I do anything right?*

But as the song changes, Ms. Kaplan turns back to me

with cheerful eyes. "Do you need a ride home, Shoshanna? I'd be happy to take you!"

"Oh, thanks! But I'm sure one of my friends can—" I stop midsentence, swallow hard, and then change course. "Actually, a ride would be great, if you don't mind."

I catch a glimpse of Jake in the mirror. He has a strange look on his face; one might even call it . . . *concerned*? But he quickly returns his eyes to his notebook.

"No problem," Ms. Kaplan smoothly responds. "I don't mind at all."

Jake and I walk in silence toward the mall entrance. It feels even colder outside after the warmth of the car, and we have to walk *all* the way around because I forgot only the south entrance is open this early in the morning. Our steps echo against the pavement, Jake's long strides and my short ones. After a couple minutes, Jake glances at me, his gaze curious. "What's up with you today?"

"What do you mean?" I ask, shoving my hands into my coat pockets, unnerved by his inspection.

"Well, you aren't talking," Jake states. "Which is strange."

The words settle for a moment, and then I surprise myself by laughing. Hard. He laughs too, and my throat catches as our eyes connect, as my eyes then travel from his smile to the curve of his jaw to his yellow-and-black flannel shirt. Only a flannel shirt. No jacket. "You do know it's winter, right?"

I ask, right as a bitter burst of wind bites against snatches of my exposed skin.

Jake raises an eyebrow. "Yes, I know it's winter."

"Well, you might want to wear a jacket."

"I'm good." He flashes me a smile so flagrantly charming it could put Noah Centineo to shame. "I run hot."

Well, I certainly feel less cold now. I look down to hide my flushed face.

"It's weird seeing the mall this empty," Jake comments as we round a corner. The south entrance is in sight, finally.

"Just wait until we get inside," I reply. "Being in the mall this early is freaky."

We revert back to silence, our feet against the pavement again the only sound. I rub my frozen nose, and he rubs his hands together before shoving them into his pockets and doing this tiny shoulder-shiver I know he's trying to hide from me. *Ugh. Boys.* I roll my eyes and rummage through my tote bag. Then I thrust a purple scarf in his direction. "Here."

He shakes his head. "I'm good."

"You're *cold*."

"Nah, I'm good."

"Your cheeks are red."

"So are yours."

"Argh!" I stop short and shout. "I swear to god, Jake Kaplan, don't be so stubborn and just take the freaking scarf!"

He stops too, and blinks at me in shock. Then suddenly

we're both laughing again, and his eyes are all bright and amused, and his cheeks are redder than before, and my heart may or may not be pounding harder than that time Geraldine forced me to see one of those Saw movies, and seriously, who gave Jake Kaplan the right to be so darn attractive? It is, truly, unfair.

"Okay," Jake relents, smile softer now. One might even call it a fond smile. Like he's *fond* of *me*. He takes my scarf and wraps it twice around his neck. "Happy?"

I rock back on my heels and appraise him. He looks cute without my scarf but even cuter with my scarf. And it's all really annoying, you know, because people shouldn't be allowed to look cute before eight a.m. when the rest of us look like stuffed animals that have been run over by a truck and then thrown through an industrial washer on the heavy-duty cycle.

"Yep," I finally say, taking a short breath. "Totally happy." My phone buzzes. Alarm number three. Time to be at Once Upon for set up. "C'mon, we're going to be late."

We hurry up and make it through the south entrance. Sure enough, the mall is deserted. A few employees roam the halls, but with most of the lights still turned off, that makes it even creepier. "I feel like I'm in one of those zombie shows," Jake says.

"'The Shopping Dead,'" I reply.

He snorts, hard.

I bristle. "Stop laughing at me."

"I'm not laughing *at* you," Jake says. "It was funny."

"Oh." I tug on a strand of hair, twisting the curl around my finger. "Well, thanks. I *am* funny. It's about time you noticed." I pause. "I just feel like usually you're laughing at me."

"Yeah, maybe," he admits. "Though to be fair, usually you're yelling at me, so . . ."

"I don't yell!"

"Shoshanna . . . really?"

I inhale quickly. I hate it how much I like it when he says my name. "I don't mean to yell," I say. "I just get overexcited."

His grin is sly. "Thanks for sharing."

I blush, deeply, and stay like that for the rest of our walk. *Ugh. Boys.*

Jake and I agree that I'll set up the chairs while he sets up the books. But when I turn to check on his progress, I find him stacking the books in a tall pyramid instead of a regular pile. "It's going to fall," I tell him.

"It's not going to fall," he replies.

Myra zooms by us, and without stopping, calls out, "It's going to fall. Redo it!"

"Told you," I say. "Just takes one customer who thinks the best copy is on the bottom to topple the whole thing. And yes, that has happened before. In retail, it's important to remember that the customer is always right except for when the customer is very, very wrong."

"Yeah, yeah, okay." Jake runs a hand through his hair. His soft, curly hair I still want to touch, like the weirdo I am. It feels like we're getting somewhere this morning—Jake and me, not Jake's hair and me. But maybe by the transitive property also Jake's hair and me. We aren't friends, per se, but we've reached a more comfortable level of animosity.

"Here." I hand him a folding chair. "You finish these. I'll fix the books."

"I can unstack books," he replies with the slightest hint of an eye-roll.

I tilt my head. "Can you, though?"

"Yes." He steps forward and goes to grab the top book. I step forward too and jump up on my tippy toes to reach the same top book.

"I've got it," he says.

"I have—"

"Oh—"

"No!" I finish.

I've always had a suspicion I'll die in some stupid way, and here it is, happening already, before I'm even old enough to buy a scratch-off lotto ticket.

The pyramid of books tumbles down. I brace my arms over my head and prepare for death, but then Jake pushes me in front of him and kind of holds himself over my head so the stack of books rains down mostly on him, while I'm curled under his chest. And it's warm in here. And instead of sweet, he smells savory today, spices and herbs I can't identify, and I wonder if my scarf will smell like him when he returns it to me, and he's breathing heavily, and my skin is all tingly, and his chest is pressed against my back, and I kind of want to lean into him and press fully against him, and—

The last book tumbles to the floor, Jake moves away, and all of that warmth evaporates. "Ow," he says as he rubs his head.

"Thank—" I cough, cheeks red, real red, outrageously red. "Thank you."

Then I look at the mess, books scattered and strewn everywhere, some opened in precarious, potential jacket-cover-ripping situations. Shame pulses through me. Myra asked us to do one thing, and we're screwing it up. *I'm* screwing it up. And that's not okay. I *do* need to think. I *do* need to grow up. I posted Geraldine's video without asking, cried wolf with an emergency at home, and now this.

"Jake," I say, throat tight as I pick up a couple of books and inspect them, praying they aren't damaged. "This is a big event for the store, and Myra needs us to do a good job. I'm going to restack these books, okay? It'll go faster, and you can do the chairs, and then we'll both get ready to greet people."

I expect protest, but Jake nods. "You're right. Okay."

I let out a little sigh of relief and then hold out my hand for a shake. Jake eyes me, like he thinks it might be a trick. Which, fair enough. But it isn't a trick. I want to do a good job for Myra, for the store, and for myself. Jake steps forward and grasps my hand. His skin is callused, and I wonder from what. My neck heats as I hold on a moment too long.

"Truce?" Jake asks.

I feel a spark at the base of my spine when his eyes meet mine. "Truce."

By the time we're finished with setup, at least two dozen customers are lined up outside the locked Once Upon doors. They shift anxiously on their feet. Some chat with friends, and some have their noses stuffed into books. I spy a lot of canvas tote bags. Ah, my people.

"That's a big crowd," Jake says.

Only Liv Childers could bring in a crowd this massive first thing in the morning, especially during the holidays. But what better time to celebrate a series called Christmas Killings? Liv is already in the store, chatting with Myra in her office, and other Once Upon employees have arrived to help shepherd customers and keep the store from falling into total chaos.

"Ready?" I ask. Jake nods, so I unlock the doors and pull them open. The customers stream inside at an alarming pace. "Like the Jews flooding out of Egypt," I observe. Jake laughs, and I fizz with pleasure.

Turns out I really like making Jake Kaplan laugh.

As more customers stream into the store, we part ways to sell books, make sure the aisles stay straight, and confirm with one person after the next that the signing will happen after the reading. The seats fill up so quickly that people are already claiming the prime standing room spots behind the last row of chairs. After I again explain the signing line policy to someone, I notice a commotion going on up front. I push through the crowd toward a man standing before the first row. His blond hair is buzzed short. A pair of sunglasses hang around his neck, and his lip juts out in annoyance. "What's this sign for?" He points to a chair with a reserved sign. "VIP or something? Special guest?"

"No, sir," I say. "That's our reserved seating for disabled customers."

"Well, I'm not disabled. But there are no other seats left, so I'm taking it."

My pulse upticks. Despite my penchant for falling face-first into it, I don't actually like confrontation. And I particularly don't like confrontation with strange men. My muscles tense as the memory of that thief in the philosophy section resurfaces.

I can't let the guy sit here. It's not right. But I need to stay calm. Not scream, not act on impulse, and also not run away. I need to handle this situation with maturity. "I'm sorry sir," I say, "but you can't sit there. As I mentioned, it's reserved for disabled customers. I hope you understand."

His white skin reddens. "So because you're disabled you get a reserved seat up front and everyone else has to show up early or stand? Doesn't sound like equality to me."

He sits down in the seat and crosses his arms, lips pressed into a firm line. I clear my throat. "Well, you see, actually it is fair because disabled people, well they—" I know this reasoning. I know it well. Myra trains us all about accessibility, from wider aisles to large-print signs to reserved seats at events. But it's like all of that knowledge and reason has left the building as I stare at this angry man.

"Sir," a voice cuts in. Jake comes up behind me. I inhale his savory scent, like fresh-baked bread with freaking rosemary or something. It eases the tension in my shoulders. *Jake* eases the tension in my shoulders. "As my coworker here has already mentioned, this seat is reserved for disabled customers. Since you've clearly said you are not disabled, I need you to move and stand in the back."

"Are you serious?" the man asks, casting his eyes around, as if waiting for other customers to agree with him. But everyone seems to be pointedly staring in any other possible direction. "Look, I'll tell you what." The man directs his focus back at us. "If a disabled person comes up and asks for the seat, I'll give it to them."

My frustration bubbles over. "That's not how this works," I say, doing everything within my power to keep my cool even though all I want to do is shout. Seriously, screw this guy who thinks the world exists to cater only to him. "Disabled people shouldn't have to constantly ask for accommodation in this world. They shouldn't have to feel uncomfortable going up to someone and asking them to move. That's my job." I keep my voice firm but calm as I level my eyes at him. "So. Move."

Jake leans closer to the man. "Now. Or we'll call security."

"This is ridiculous," the man mutters, but he gets out of the chair. "You just lost my business. I hope you're both happy."

"We're ecstatic," I mutter once he's out of earshot, shoving his way through the crowd and leaving the store.

Now that he's gone, I notice how fast my pulse is racing, adrenaline pounding through my veins, hands shaking lightly at my sides. I turn to Jake and realize he must feel as much rage as me by how hard his jaw is clenched. I swear a vein even ticks in his forehead. "That guy was a jerk," he finally says.

"The jerkiest," I reply, letting out a shaky breath. "Thanks for the help, by the way."

"Sure." Jake's stance relaxes, and so does mine, and I want to say something else to him, something more, but then Myra's office door opens, and she heads toward us with Liv Childers at her side. I'm glad she wasn't here to witness that guy. And I'm surprised, but glad, I was able to handle it without screaming or stealing someone's walkie to use the

PA system. And as Myra and Liv settle at the table and begin the panel, a woman with a canvas tote bag and a slight limp walks into the store, notices the RESERVED sign, and sits down in relief.

Chapter Ten

"I'm exhausted," Jake says.

"I'm Shoshanna," I reply automatically.

He snorts. "Nice dad joke."

"Thanks." We walk into the break room and promptly collapse into chairs. My head feels a solid five pounds heavier than yesterday, and I crack a giant yawn. "*Oof*. I'm exhausted too. But also, that event was awesome. We sold so many books!"

The event *was* awesome, well, after the incident with the jerkiest of jerks. Liv Childers was charming and audacious—totally titillating the crowd with real life stories of gore. Everyone was in a good mood, not minding the two-hour—yes, two-hour—line to get their books signed. Jake and I used so many QR codes we're definitely in the lead for the competition, which hopefully means *I'm* in the lead for the competition.

Thankfully Arjun and Sophie-Anne were assigned to

break down the chairs and clean up because Jake and I need a rest after that marathon. Myra even said we could take a full hour for lunch. I glance at Jake, who scratches his jaw and blinks sleepily at me like a kid who just woke up after a road-trip nap. *Cute.* I smile a little smile and decide to offer him an olive branch. "Hey," I say. "Want to join me in the food court? I'll probably grab lunch with my—"

Oh. Wait.

I can't grab lunch with my friends. In the exhausted haze of a frenzied event, I almost forgot my two best friends currently hate me. I clamp my mouth shut and look down at the table.

I can feel Jake's curious gaze on me. "What was that?"

"Hmm?" I ask.

"You did the same thing in the car earlier. Are you fighting with your friends?"

I force a laugh and nonchalant tone. "Okay, Sherlock, nose in your own business, please." He's silent in response. I inspect the table. Illustrations are scratched into the wood. Going by the Satanic symbols, I guess they're probably the work of Sophie-Anne and Arjun.

Jake screeches his chair back and stands up. I assume he's going to leave me alone in the break room, but then he asks, "Want a sandwich?"

Um. What?

I look up at him. "Jake Kaplan, are you offering to *make me a sandwich?*"

His eyes flicker with amusement. "Sure. Why not? I'm making one for myself."

"Well, what kind of sandwich?" I sit up a little. "Not ham, right?"

"Not to worry. No ham, Shoshanna Greenberg." I glow a little at his response. "It's like a PB and J but better."

I think of those almonds and trust that Jake can do a PB&J justice as well. "Okay, I like PB and J. Ooh! You know what goes great with a PB and J? Chocolate milk. I wonder if . . ."

Jake laughs. I'm pretty sure it's one of those laugh *at* me occasions, but that's okay. I don't think he means it in a bad way. Chocolate milk is delicious. Little kids have good taste.

"I don't have chocolate milk," he replies, "but the sandwich will taste good on its own. I promise." He moves around the break room, pulling ingredients out of his locker, washing his hands, and then assembling two sandwiches. I try not to watch him the whole time like a creep and instead look at the flyers on our bulletin board, one for a bake sale and one for a Motel/Hotel concert, some EDM band from Athens that Tanya likes. But then I hear wrinkling and pay attention to Jake as he opens a small bag of Ruffles and meticulously places the chips on top of the spread with the precision of a surgeon. He then puts the second piece of bread on top and, *crunch*.

"Interesting ingredient," I comment.

He brings two plates over to the table. "You'll like it. Promise."

I raise an eyebrow and assess my sandwich. "So what's in here?"

"One layer of hazelnut spread, one layer of almond butter, one layer of pomegranate jam, and of course, Ruffles."

"Of course." I nod, then pick up the sandwich. Jake pretends to look down at his plate, but I can feel him watching me out of the corner of his eye, a bit of tension in the air, kind of like when I share my writing with someone and pretend to not pay attention to every minute shift in their expression.

Okay. No pressure. It's just a sandwich. I lean forward and take a good-size bite, teeth crunching through the chips and three layers of spread, and wow. Like, wow. Salty and sweet. Soft and crispy. I chew and chew and swallow, then look up and say—okay, shout, "What the heck, Jake!"

His mask of confidence slips, his brows furrowed into worry. "What?"

"Why is this so good? What kind of sandwich nobel laureate are you?"

Jake's lips quirk, and then he laughs, scratching the back of his neck in this painfully adorable self-conscious way. "Thanks, Shoshanna."

"Seriously, though," I continue, nibbling off a miniature bite because I need to savor this flavor. "This is delicious, and

those almonds were delicious, and you always smell deli—"
My cheeks flaming, I stop talking.

But it wasn't in time.

Jake tilts his head, his smile growing by the second. "You think I smell delicious?"

"Uh." I clear my throat and look anywhere but at him, which means looking at a water stain on the ceiling and also a spot that looks suspiciously like black mold. Someone should probably tell Myra about it. "Anyway . . . so do you cook a lot or something?"

"Yeah, I do." Jake spares me from death by utter mortification and moves on from the me-smelling-him topic. "I enjoy it a lot—baking, too." His words are carefully picked, like he's trying to hide his level of enthusiasm, but honestly, who has to worry about dorking out and carefully picking words around me?

"When did you start?" I ask, nibbling another bite of god's gift to taste buds.

"As a kid." Jake picks up his own sandwich and manages to eat while talking without looking gross, an impressive feat. "Mom worked long hours. And we didn't have one of those rich-kid-in-a-teen-movie fully stocked fridges. So I experimented with what we did have. You know, Kraft mac 'n' cheese but with Parmesan and chili flakes. Or Cheerios with cinnamon milk and bananas. Just whatever I could come up with. It was fun. And then I started working at Gary's."

"Gary's?" I ask. Dang it. My sandwich is almost gone. I wonder if Jake has enough ingredients for seconds.

"It's a diner, near Canton Highway. I was hired as a busboy a few years ago, but I always asked Gary to let me help out in the kitchen. I'd ask questions and suggest ingredients . . . and add seasonings to dishes when he wasn't looking." Jake pauses. "I might have been annoying."

"Can't relate to being annoying," I say. "Nope, not at all."

Jake grins right at me, and my stomach flutters. *Concentrate on the sandwich, Shoshanna.* "At some point," he continues, "I annoyed Gary into giving me a chance, and now I cook and tinker with the menu. And I do a lot of the baking. That's the notebook I carry around, recipe ideas. Of course, I still bus tables, too."

I scrunch my eyebrows. "But you work here."

"Yeah. Gary can only offer me so many hours, and money is tight at home, so—"

"I get it," I say quickly. "I mean, maybe I don't *get* it, get it. But I kind of understand. Like I need my job to fix Barbra Streisand—not the singer," I clarify, when Jake gives me a really confused look. "My car, Barbra Streisand, she needs a repair. And I asked Myra for extra hours next year, but she doesn't have them, and I don't really know what to do. . . ." I pause, thoughts clicking together. "Oh."

"Oh, what?" Jake asks, picking up the last bite of his sandwich.

Guilt and embarrassment claw at me. I am so not smart. If Jake is working two jobs, he probably needs the bonus money as much if not more than I do. And here I thought he mostly wanted to win to annoy me. Wow. And the award for most self-centered assumption-making jerk goes to . . .

"What?" Jake asks again.

I fidget with the chain of my necklace and look down at my feet, which hover half an inch above the scuffed-up floor because short person. "So," I say. "I need that bonus money to fix Barbra, but maybe you need it for, I don't know, the electric bill or something—not that you *do* need it for that!" *Foot in mouth, Shoshanna. Foot. In. Mouth.* "I'm not assuming either way, which is my point. Um. Like." *Has my face been red this entire conversation?* "Sorry. Um. The point is that I've been a jerk to you. And I'm sorry."

I chance glancing up at Jake. His eyes are so soft I could melt right into my wobbly break-room chair. When he speaks, I can feel my pulse racing lightly under my skin. "You haven't been a jerk," he replies. "Well, at least no more than I've been one." Jake pauses then. A *long* pause, like with an inhale and everything, like he's really gathering up the courage for the next part. "I was not the nicest person in the world to you on my first day."

"You weren't?" I ask. "Actually, I know you weren't. You weren't the nicest."

Jake laughs. It's a hard laugh but a quick one, and when

it's over, he looks at me. Really looks at me. I fidget under his gaze and pray for him to break the silence even though I'm not really a Jew who prays so much as a Jew who loves a good kugel and a lightly toasted sesame-seed bagel with white fish. Finally, he shifts back in his chair and says, "I wanted to do a good job so Myra would give me more hours. I was focused on that and not—"

"Making friends?" I ask, then put on my best reality-TV-star voice. "I'm not here to make friends."

"Yeah." Jake grins. "Something like that. So, I'm sorry too." He runs a hand through his curls. "Want to tell me what's going on with your friends? I've been told I'm a good listener."

"Have you?" I counter with a light smile.

"Yeah," he says in all sincerity, and I feel approximately eight thousand tingles in response.

I tug on a strand of my hair, unsure and nervous. But then somehow, maybe because of my exhaustion or Jake's eyes or this delicious Michelin-star PB&J, it all spills out—everything about my moms fighting and my friends being angry with me, everything about each one of my impulsive screw-ups. When I finish, I feel flustered and out of breath but also relieved, like just admitting it all has eased some of the pressure.

"That's really tough," Jake says. His gaze, focused right on me, is so earnest I have to lean back in my chair and twist my fingers together. "But it sounds like you know what you did wrong, which is great, because now you can apologize and fix it."

"Yeah." I nod, but my nerves are knotted tight. "But what if they don't accept my apology? What if they don't like me anymore?"

"Oh." His eyes are amused. "I'd find it very hard to believe someone could stop liking you, Shoshanna."

My heart jumps hard like it's trying to make a slam dunk in my chest. The teasing question comes out before I can stop it, "Does that mean *you* like me?"

His smile is sly. "Well, I certainly don't hate you."

For some reason, those words sound like a profession of love. I bite my nail to hide my own smile, then say, "I certainly don't hate you either, Jake Kaplan."

My phone buzzes, and I glance down, hoping for a text from my friends or my moms. But it's not from any of them. My stomach drops as I look back up at Jake and say, "Myra wants to see us in her office."

My thoughts race as we walk to Myra's office in silence. I thought the event went well today, but what if I'm wrong? Is Myra going to ban us from the competition? Was it the book pyramid? Did she notice it fall?

Even though her office door is open, Jake knocks on the frame, and we wait for Myra to call out, "Come in," before we step into the room.

"You wanted to see us?" Jake asks. His posture is stiff, uncertain, like he's wearing a three-piece suit instead of his flannel. He must feel nervous as well. After all, he just told me how important this job is to him. What if neither of us can win the bonus?

I scoot closer to Jake than usual, close enough that I can feel the heat off his body, close enough to smell the lingering scent of rosemary that I now know comes from baking. It's nice, standing this close to him, and it eases the tension gripped around my muscles.

"Yes, I did," Myra says. I steal a breath as she clicks something on her computer and then slides off her pair of reading glasses. "I have some news. As you know, there are only two days left in the competition, so I wanted to let you know that you are both tied for first place."

Shock pulses through me. I was not expecting *that*. "We're . . . tied?"

Jake seems just as surprised but with a much different reaction. A small smile flits to his lips. He tries to hide it by covering his mouth with a cough, then not-so-coolly asks, "Exactly tied?"

"Exactly tied," Myra confirms. She taps her fingers against the arm of her chair. "I'm impressed. Didn't think I'd see the numbers get this high, even with the Childers event. But you both have been putting in a lot of hours and working hard on sales. Y'all are doing a great job."

"Awesome," I say weakly. Relief should be flooding through me right now. I wanted to prove I'm good at my job, that I'm a responsible employee, and that's what I've done. But instead it feels like my almost surefire chance of winning the money to fix Barbra has slipped to 50 percent.

We don't have the money, Shoshanna, Mom said. *You'll need to figure this out on your own.* But what if I can't? Barbra is dead in the driveway. What if I have to beg for rides not just for the next few days but for the next few months, the tension at home growing with each request? I want to make things better for my family, happier, like they used to be. I want to solve problems, not make them worse.

I tug on a strand of hair as Myra congratulates us again, and then Jake and I leave her office in silence. We walk side by side, aimlessly toward the back of the store. As we approach a shelf of box sets, Jake grabs my hand to stop us both. His hand drops away immediately after, but my skin still tingles from the short contact.

"Look," he says.

And so I look at him.

I look at his lips and then his eyes and then for the first time I notice he has a crooked eyebrow. His left one kind of arches up at the end. And since when can eyebrows be attractive? But I guess they can be. I am attracted to Jake Kaplan's eyebrow, and that's something I'm going to have to live with for the rest of my life. "I know this money is important for both of us," Jake continues, "but I feel like we're getting along. I like you—"

My pulse skips. He likes me? As in *likes* me, likes me?

"—you're funny and different, and I think we could be friends."

Oh. Right.

Just one like. Not a *like* like. Because people don't *like* like the funny and different girl, the loud girl who puts her foot in her mouth and then keeps talking, the weird, sensitive girl who wants to cry because her mom went out to buy milk but we already had milk. I clear my throat and try to keep my voice upbeat as I reply, "Sure. We could be friends."

"Good." Jake smiles. As always, it's a great smile. I genuinely believe he has a shot at a very specific type of modeling for oral healthcare trade magazines. But at the moment, my stomach is too tense for smile-induced butterflies. "So let's not turn this tie into a bad thing. We'll both compete, and the best bookseller will win. Can we do that?"

I wish his words were something different. But being friends with Jake is better than fighting with Jake, and I know the next few days will be infinitely better if this is a friendly competition. "We can do that," I agree.

He holds out his hand. "Friends?"

When I touch his callused skin again, an image flashes through my mind, Jake baking bread from scratch, kneading the dough with intense concentration. My neck heats as my eyes find his, and I say, "Friends."

* * *

Lola Roman, Daniel's girlfriend, has pink hair, wears thick glasses, and is four feet eleven and a half inches tall, which makes her exactly half an inch shorter than me, which means I love standing next to her. I also love standing next to her because she always carries extra gum in her purse and doesn't make that big dramatic sigh some people make when you ask for a piece. Also, she's a fountain of random trivia that always entertains.

"Did you know peacocks have a wingspan of up to six feet?" Lola asks as we roam the audiobook section.

"So they're bigger than us?" I ask.

"Well, many things are bigger than *us*, Shoshanna. Ooh! I love this one." Lola snatches a thriller off the shelf. "Gave me epic creeps. Didn't sleep well for a week. It was awesome!"

Lola hands it to me as she continues to peruse the shelves. Having low vision, she's an audiobook fiend. I asked her to endorse some choices for customer recommendations because I need to round out my full book knowledge if I'm going to beat Jake and his tablet quiz. I want to like audiobooks, but I always zone out after thirteen point eight seconds. I have trouble listening in class, too. If I'm not reading something, eyes on the page, it's like the information goes in one ear and out the other. Or, it might not even go in the ear to begin with.

"Ooh! This one is a great romance. Very steamy." Lola

raises her eyebrows up and down. She has a tiny silver hoop threaded through her right brow.

She passes me the book as Daniel sweeps in behind us. "What's very steamy?" he asks, and then grabs the book, *An Extraordinary Seduction*, out of my hands. "Ooh, yeah, this one was steamy. We liked it."

"*We?*" I let out a short laugh. "Y'all listen to erotic romance novels together?"

Daniel wraps an arm around Lola. She leans into his shoulder, her tinted pink hair falling down between them. "It's a great couple's activity," Lola explains. "You know, movies are expensive these days." She says "these days" like she's ninety, not nineteen.

"How are things going with the family in town?" I ask Daniel. He's almost been working fewer hours than during the school year, and I miss seeing his face around the store all the time.

"Overall good," he answers. "Though my parents are peak stressed. They drive themselves crazy trying to be perfect hosts."

I grin. "I love your parents." His parents are Once Upon regulars, especially his mom, who has become a graphic-novel enthusiast like her son. I love when they visit the store. They're funny and friendly and all-around awesome. Just like the son they raised.

It's like all my friends have these perfect sitcom parents,

you know, the kind that are always there when you get home from school and have dinner on the table every night, and you all sit down together and they ask about your day and really want to hear the answer. Cheyenne's dad always wants to spend time with her, and her mom does as well. She's onboard for all of Cheyenne's hobbies, even beekeeping despite being terrified of bees, whatever it takes to spend time with her daughter.

And Geraldine's mom practices new makeup techniques with her, and once a month they cook a bunch of food together for their church. And I always see Geraldine's phone light up with texts from her dad—pictures of random hedgehogs because they have an obsession with hedgehogs and believe they're cuter than every other animal in existence, including, yes, dogs.

And I'm sure their parents aren't actually perfect sitcom parents because no one is perfect, but they're around and involved and care, and my moms were always like that too. They attended all of my debate tournaments, until I quit in seventh grade due to a sudden case of puberty-induced stage fright. We went to synagogue together every other month so we wouldn't look bad to the rabbi. And every now and then Mama would say "*Screw it*, let's have cake for dinner," and we'd head to Delights Diner, where Mama would get carrot cake, Mom would get chocolate supreme cake, and I'd forgo cake for the best slice of apple pie in the world.

But we don't do anything together lately, not even Latke-palooza. And when we *are* together, the room crackles with tension so intense it makes my skin crawl. And I don't like it. I don't like it at all. I want my sitcom family back.

"Hey," Daniel says right after the store bell chimes. "Isn't that *your* mom?"

"No," I dismiss him, but glance toward the door anyway. "It's only four. She's at work, and she wouldn't—"

But there she is, standing by the entrance, like I summoned her from my thoughts. She's wearing her favorite slim navy trousers and this vintage white blouse I've always loved. She looks cool, mature, and hip, and I suddenly feel self-conscious of my daffodil-print dress even though it's totally cute and I snagged it on mega-sale.

"That's her, right?" Daniel asks.

I nod. "Yeah."

"Wow!" Lola says. "Y'all look so similar!"

I think I'm supposed to glow with pleasure at that, but instead it only makes my muscles tense. There's no doubt that Mom and I look alike. On the weekends, when she wears her favorite old jeans and concert T-shirts, we'll occasionally get asked if we're sisters—in the way that people actually think it, not in the gross-old-man-trying-to-compliment-a-woman-for-not-being-old kind of way. But I don't glow with pleasure. I only twist my fingers together. What is she doing at Once Upon? Did I do something wrong? She wouldn't yell at me here, would she?

I'm frozen, rooted in place, but I can feel the weird looks that Daniel and Lola are boring into the back of my head. Okay, a normal person would go up and greet their mother. Okay. "Um, I'll see you guys later," I tell them, then force one lead foot up and then the next until I make it over to Mom.

She registers me when I'm a few feet away, and then she does the strangest thing. She smiles. A little bit of an uncomfortable smile, but still. It's the effort that counts, right?

"Hey, Mom," I say. "What's, um, why are you here?"

She seems to look just past me as she pushes her hair behind her ears, like she can't quite meet my eyes. "I saw Barbra in the driveway," she answers. "I thought I'd give you a ride home. You get off soon, right?"

"Oh, yeah." The smallest bit of tension releases from my shoulders. "Yeah, in ten minutes."

"Great!" Mom clasps her hands together. Her wedding ring glints under the store lights, an heirloom from Mama's grandmother. "I'll meet you here when you're ready."

"Great." I'm not sure what to say next so I just add, "Thanks," and leave with a quick wave. *A wave?*

Nine minutes later, I'm in the break room gathering my things. Jake walks in, and I chirp, "Oh, good!"

He tilts his head with an inquisitive smile. "Shoshanna Greenberg, are you happy to see me?"

"Don't get ahead of yourself." I laugh. "My mom is going

to drive me home, so I don't need a ride today. Thank your mom for me, though!"

"Hey, that's a good sign, right?" he asks. "That your mom is here?"

I tug on my tote bag. "I think so?"

"Hope so. Just let us know if you need a ride. Anytime."

"Thanks, Jake." I pause. "It's weird we're friends now."

He laughs. "Yeah."

"I like it though," I nervously admit.

His eyes seem to soften at my words, which makes my stomach flip. "Me too."

I give him a quick smile and then, cheeks warming, slip by him and out the break room door.

The car ride home is awkward. Conversation is surface level—I swear at one point we keep the weather chat going for a straight five minutes. I pick at my nails and stare out the window as we get closer to home. Christmas decorations line the streets, houses decked out in twinkling lights, yards covered with Santas and reindeers and fake snow. It looks like a storybook, cozy and warm. I pull my coat tighter around me.

We get home and step inside to the smell of roasted garlic. "I made soup!" Mama calls out from the kitchen. "Thought we could all have dinner together."

"Thank you, Alex," Mom calls back.

We slip off our shoes and shrug out of our jackets before heading into the kitchen. Mama finishes seasoning the soup, while Mom takes dishes from the cabinet. I grab spoons and napkins and help set the table, and soon we're all sitting with bowls of tomato soup and garlic bread. The scene is so domestic, so *normal*, I feel disoriented.

"Tastes great," I lie after taking a sip. Not because it tastes bad but because I feel too apprehensive for things like taste buds to work. To be honest, the soup tastes like anxiety.

Mama smiles at me. The sleeves of her thermal shirt are pushed up to her elbows, and she's still wearing a gingham apron. "Thanks, darling."

"So." Mom clears her throat and attempts a smile as well. She pulls her hair back into her after-work bun, a messy affair with serious Albert Einstein vibes. "Shoshanna, your mama and I wanted to have a chat with you. We . . ." She scratches her ear, then puts her hand down, then picks it back up to fiddle with her soup soon. "We want to apologize."

I was about to take a bite of garlic bread, but now my mouth feels too dry. An apology? I was expecting a lot of things, but I wasn't expecting that. "Um. You do?"

"Yes." Mama takes in a little breath as she looks at me. "Sweetheart, we weren't being mature either. We shouldn't have been fighting like that. And we certainly shouldn't have made it feel like *you* needed to fix anything. You're our daughter. We love you. We take care of you. You can take care of us when we're old and wrinkled. Well—" She laughs. "More wrinkled than now."

"Oh." Moisture pricks at my eyes as the words settle in. "So . . . you're okay, then? You're going to stop fighting?"

They exchange a look, and my quick relief fades. Mama gives a small nod before Mom replies, "We're sorry for the screaming and for missing Latkepalooza. That was unfair of us. But we don't know if—" Her voice breaks a little. She clears her throat and stirs her soup. "Your mama and I have some issues we need to talk about. We found a therapist, and we're going to attend sessions with her after the New Year. We'll just have to see if . . . if this is still working."

This, as in their marriage.

There's a long silence. I feel like we're all trying not to cry. Or maybe that's just me.

Mama leans across the table and squeezes my hand. "Shoshanna, we love you. No matter what happens between us, we love you. And we'll be better about the fighting, and we're sorry we missed Latkepalooza. We understand why you did what you did, but you have to promise us there's not going to be a repeat incident. We were really worried."

"We know you wanted to help," Mom says. "But there's a difference between asking to help and interfering. If something we're doing is affecting you negatively, talk to us about it. Don't keep it to yourself and then try to fix it behind our backs. Because that probably won't end well. Okay?"

"Okay," I say, and then look down at my soup. This conversation has been so short, steam still rises off of the surface—and yet—everything has changed.

"We love you," Mom says.

"We'll always love you," Mama agrees.

The way they keep repeating those words makes it feel like they're breaking up with me. And there's nothing I can do about it. I just have to wait and see if my life is going to be flipped inside out. I stir my soup and say, "I love you too."

Chapter Eleven

If my life were a movie, this is the point where I would make a grand romantic gesture. I'd run through the airport. I'd confess my love on the Jumbotron at a baseball game. I'd sprinkle a hundred rose petals on the bed.

But my life isn't a movie. And it's not baseball season, and Geraldine and Cheyenne would probably find it weird if I sprinkled rose petals on their beds. So instead I ask them to meet me at the mall half an hour before work, and surprisingly, thankfully, they agree. I walk up to them with penance in hand—the chocolate chip banana bread muffins I made last night after my moms retreated to their bedroom.

My stomach churns as I sit at the table across from my friends and place the bag down. The food court is empty, and I can hear my heartbeat in my ears. "Hi," I say softly.

Cheyenne's sweater is bubblegum pink. Geraldine's nails are coated in moss-green polish. My palms are sweating like a block of ice in a sauna.

I nudge the bag forward. Cheyenne takes it and inspects with a small smile. Geraldine tugs on her shirtsleeve. My hands squeeze so tight, my knuckles turn white. I want my friends back. I also vaguely want to barf.

In the ninth grade, we all went to a Halloween party together. Cheyenne got an invite from a friend on the year-book staff. She was the only freshman on the staff because, like everything else, she had a natural knack for Photoshop. Geraldine got an invite from the girls on her softball team. And I got an invite as the plus one for my two best friends.

It was a *real* Halloween party. Full of upperclassmen, loud, thumping music, a barely lit basement, and flavored vodka in cups of off-brand Coke. No scary-movie mara-thons. And definitely no trick-or-treating. I dressed up as Hermione, regular Hermione, not a gross sexpot version. Cheyenne dressed as Tahani from *The Good Place*, all five feet eight inches of her looking glorious in an elegant ball gown her mom wore to some black-tie gala years before. And Ger-aldine dressed as Rosa Díaz from *Brooklyn Nine-Nine* with an on-point impression. She rocked the hell out of that leather jacket, while my Hogwarts robe was obviously intended for someone six inches taller.

The second we walked into the party, I felt out of place—too young, too short, hair too frizzy even for Granger. I didn't belong. I didn't fit. The one thing I had going for me was the ability to crack a good joke, but it's hard to impress with faultless wordplay when the music is so loud it makes you regret the fact that you have ears. But Cheyenne grabbed one of my hands and Geraldine grabbed the other, and they shepherded me through the crowd, flitting us from one group to the next, and by the end of the night I'd played my first round of beer pong (with La Croix), joined a rambunctious game of Truth or Dare, and made approximately fifty new friends.

Except I didn't need those fifty new friends. Not really. Because that night I realized I already had the two best friends in the world.

What if my mistake was too big? What if I lose them?

"Um." I look down at my lap and squeeze my hands harder, nails digging into my palms. I'm not actually Hermione Granger. There's no time turner to go back and fix my screwup. I have to apologize and hope we can move forward. My pulse jumps as I begin to apologize. "I'm sorry. I know what I did was wrong. And I won't do anything like that again. I won't interfere. And I e-mailed Lucille Tifton last night and explained the entire situation. She hasn't responded yet, but hopefully she will. And—" I swallow hard, blood thrumming in my veins. "I really miss you guys, and I hope you can forgive me. I messed up, and I'm sorry. Please don't hate me. Please."

I wait for a long, painful stretched-out pause. I wait for anger or cool dismissal.

But when I look up, I find Cheyenne's eyes are soft. She leans across the table and takes my hand with a quick squeeze. "Shosh, we don't *hate* you."

My voice wobbles. "You don't?"

"Of course not," Geraldine says. "You messed up. But, like, people mess up. And you apologized. And also we love you."

They're both looking at me with concern now, eyes tender, and before I can stop it, I break into tears. Because of course I freaking do. I furiously wipe them away as my cheeks burn. "Sorry," I say, only crying harder as I continue, "I know it's not an excuse, but my moms have been fighting lately, and I was so stressed out, and I just wanted to fix everything. For them and for you. Because you're amazing, and I wanted to show you that, but I went about it the wrong way. I know that now. And I was just so scared I was going to lose you guys. I love you both so much. And I thought you hated me."

And then, the weirdest thing happens: Cheyenne's eyes water, and tears start running down her face, and then Geraldine starts crying too, and Cheyenne is saying, "What are you even talking about? We love you so much," and Geraldine is saying, "Oh my god, this eyeliner isn't waterproof. We love you, Shoshanna. Forever."

And they tell me how much they love me and that they're there for me no matter what, and I fill them in about everything with my moms and how I'm scared they might get divorced, and there's nothing I can do, and we're all crying, hard, and then suddenly we're all laughing, even harder, and we're making an enormous spectacle of ourselves as employees slowly make their way into the mall to find three teenage girls having simultaneous breakdowns in the middle of an empty food court.

"Shosh." Geraldine manages to speak coherently first. "You are freaking hilarious and smart and kind. What you did was wrong, but I know it came from a good place. I know how lucky I am to have you as a friend." She rubs her nose. "Geez, does anyone have a tissue?"

Cheyenne passes her a napkin and then says, "I hope these muffins taste good with snot."

"Adds that umami flavor," I say, and we all break into laughter again. Eventually, we lean back into our chairs in slap-happy exhaustion. I feel such immense relief. "In the future, I promise to only offer help, not to interfere. Okay?"

"Okay," Geraldine agrees.

"And we can help you, too, you know," Cheyenne adds. "Like with rides—RIP Barbra—or with the bookselling competition or whatever."

"Thanks," I say.

And then—an idea sparks.

Cheyenne *could* help with the competition. A smile draws to my lips. "Cheyenne, my best friend."

"Yeah?"

"Daughter of Santa . . ."

"Oh. Oh, definitely not." She shakes her head, picking up on what I'm after. "No way."

"You said *any favor*!"

"What is it?" Geraldine asks.

"Please not this," Cheyenne says.

"Definitely this." I put my hand on her shoulder and stare into her beautiful brown eyes. "I could use a Christmas miracle."

Cheyenne sighs. "Oy vey."

The copy machine in the stock room is one step from deceased. I'm pretty sure it's been here for longer than Once Upon, a remnant from the VHS media store that lived here before us. Take that, technology. Books outliving you once again! Huzzah!

Printing a hundred fliers on this dinosaur machine is a slow and painful task, and the stock room is freezer-section-of-the-grocery-store cold. I jump from foot to foot while I wait and scroll through a Time Stands Still fanfic and text with Cheyenne and Geraldine, making plans for New Year's Eve, which, other than Christmas, is the first time in weeks we'll all be off work at the same time. I'm smiling throughout the whole conversation. Who knew having a breakdown in a food court could be so good for your serotonin levels? I guess it was silly of me to think they'd just stop being my friends, but that's the thing about feelings, whether they're silly or not, they are totally freaking real.

The last flyer prints, and I hug the warm stack close to my chest. *Mmm, toasty.* Then I open the stock room door and bump straight into a solid form. A *very* solid form covered in flannel.

"Hey there," Jake says. "Morning."

I rock back on my heels and look up at his easy grin. My skin flushes. Darn it. Did he get even more attractive overnight? Do people have attractiveness growth spurts like height growth spurts? "Hi," I squeak out.

"What are those?" His eyes are on my flyers.

I bite back a smile and lower the papers so they're down by my thigh. "Nothing important. Hey, can I grab a ride to work again tomorrow? Only if it's not a problem."

"Sure," he answers, then, "as long as you tell me what those papers are for."

"Jake, are you blackmailing me? With a ride? From your mother?"

He fake winces. "Not a good look?"

"Not a great one!"

He laughs and then ducks his head forward in a nod. "Of course you can have a ride tomorrow, Shoshanna. "

"Thanks." I tug on my Star of David necklace. "Also, there are muffins in the break room. No judging my baking skills, though. We aren't all professionals."

"I'm sure they'll be delicious."

Say "delicious" again. I squelch that thought, then rush past him without a goodbye and head toward the front of the store. And the awkward-exit award goes to . . .

The aisles hum with content customers. They browse the shelves, thumb through books, and chat with their shopping companions. One girl even sits on the floor, nose tucked into a novel, a stack of five more sitting on the floor next to her. God, I love people who love books.

"Someone's on a mission," Daniel comments as I near the front doors. He's straightening our small display of Funko Pops, something I rarely spend my hard-earned money on, with the exception of once succumbing to the cuteness of Baby Groot.

I *am* on a mission with these flyers, so I'm tempted to shout out a quick response and leave, but I pause because I miss Daniel. Most of the year, my workday consists of puttering around the store with him, picking out new favorite covers, talking about our writing, setting up carefully curated tables on increasingly niche topics. My favorite table this summer was titled "Books that Start with Murder and end with a 'W.'" The display did well, too! But this holiday season has been hectic as heck. Nonstop bookselling and customer wrangling and no time for murder displays. But there should *always* be some time for my work husband.

I stop next to Daniel and help him with the Funko Pops, straightening a line of Captain Marvels. "I am on a mission," I say. "I'm trying to win the bonus."

"You and Jake still at it?" He puts Shuri and Nakia next to each other. Marvel is seriously dominating the Funko Pop game. "Give him a chance, Shosh. He's a cool guy. Even Arjun likes him. I saw them playing checkers in the break room yesterday."

I let the mental image of Arjun playing checkers wash over me for a second before replying, "I'll have you know that we are friends now. The burned bridged has been repaired, and we are two peas in a pod."

"Okay, sure. So why the rush? And what are those papers?"

I narrow my eyes and inspect Daniel. Can I trust him? He and Jake have gotten chummy pretty darn fast. "Just some flyers," I say, keeping it vague to be safe. "Trying to bring in more customers."

My phone buzzes. Cheyenne said she loved me more than anything but would only stay in Santa's Workshop for five minutes and not a second longer. "Ah, I've got to go! Will you still be working later?"

"Yep!" Daniel smiles and holds up a Squidward Funko Pop. "I always felt like this guy was misunderstood."

I grin. "See you soon, weirdo."

Then I rush out of the store and speed-walk down the

hall. The holiday music plays at full blast, and the corridors are jam-packed. Navigating these crowds should be an Olympic sport. I make it to Santa's Workshop in at least silvermedal time and then crane my neck left and right, trying to spot Cheyenne. Eventually I realize why it's so hard to find her: She's in disguise, scarf bundled up to her mouth and dark sunglasses covering her eyes.

"That's a good look," I say as I approach. "You could wear it to prom."

"Ha, ha, ha."

"You mean 'ho, ho, ho'?"

Cheyenne manages to both groan and laugh. "Shoshanna, you are truly something else."

"I know, right?" I grin. "Now let's go see Santa!"

Cheyenne shakes her head. "I cannot believe I agreed to this."

I don't totally understand what the big deal is. Aren't we a bit old to be embarrassed by the existence of our parents? But as established, feelings are feelings, so I'll make this as quick as possible. We weave through the crowd gathered around Santa's Workshop. There's a massive line of people waiting in an airport-like maze of ropes, kids tugging on parents' hands and parents pacifying them with candy because more sugar is exactly what this situation needs.

I spy Cheyenne's dad as we approach. Two kids stand in front of him, and Mr. Herman gives a hearty laugh as the picture is snapped. I imagine he drinks a lot of hot water and lemon after these long days. Or maybe hot cocoa. We make it to the side of the front of the line, and a few people shoot us paranoid looks. Yep, sorry y'all, it's exactly what you think. We're about to cut in front of you.

I clench the bundle of fliers. I don't have a fancy Buzzfeed-type quiz like Jake, so I need something to stack the competition odds in my favor. Hopefully Santa will help with that. An elf eyes us as we scoot closer to the stage. I give him my friendliest, most Shoshanna smile as I say, "Hello!"

"There's a line," the elf replies, and by "elf," I mean "man in his fifties wearing a pair of elf ears and smelling like the cigarette he probably just smoked outside." Super kid-friendly. Totally fine.

I keep my smile pasted on. "Yes, we know there's a line, but we're here to see her father."

"Shoshanna!" Cheyenne gasps. "Keep it down."

I step closer to the elf. God, that smell is pungent. Never in my life will I understand the appeal of sucking on a bunch of bitter tar.

"Her father?" the elf asks in a deadpan voice. "Like Father Christmas? Ha, ha. Nice one. What? You gonna prank him or something? Get out of here, you two."

I glance back at Cheyenne and give her a look. She sighs but then steps forward with the confidence of a beleaguered member of the royal family. "No pranks." She lowers her sunglasses to the tip of her nose. "Santa is my actual father."

I snort. Hard.

"Are you sure you're right in the head there, lady?" the elf asks.

"I hate everything," Cheyenne mutters. But then she smiles. And it's a dazzling smile, an exact match of her dad's. She brightens her voice as she speaks to the man-elf. "The man playing Santa is my father, and we need to have a quick word with him. It won't take more than a few minutes. I promise."

"There's a line," the elf repeats.

"You mentioned," I say. This conversation is going in circles. Time for brute force. I take Cheyenne's hand and push past the man-elf and toward the stage. "We'll just be a minute! Promise!" And then we also push past the grandmother-elf snapping pictures and the woman-elf ushering two kids off the stage, and then we're up on the platform right in front of Father Cheyenne himself.

"Ho, ho—Shoshanna?" He stops mid-belly-chant and peers at me in surprise.

"Hey, Santa!" I wave. "How ya doing? Hope those gifts are going to get delivered on time, or there will be many upset gentiles. Now, I know I'm a Jew, but I was wondering if you could do me a favor."

Mr. Herman looks confused, and I worry I did the thing where I talk way too fast like an auctioneer, which maybe I should consider as a possible career path. I took one of those career aptitude tests in ninth grade, and I swear to hashem, the results said *inconclusive*. My teacher told me it was a good thing—it meant I was fit for many fields of work, but I felt like that was real stretch from a real desperate teacher. I was okay with the inconclusive result, though. I don't understand why you need to know what to do for the rest of your life when you're in high school.

"A favor . . . ," Mr. Herman repeats, finally catching up. "What favor do you have in mind. Oh, and hello, daughter of mine. No hug for your dad?"

Cheyenne dutifully shuffles forward and hugs him. "I can't believe you're doing this," she mutters.

"Volunteering for a good cause?" he asks.

"Please, there are, like, eight million ways to volunteer during the holidays. You had to pick the one place where you can spy on me."

"Oh, darling, I'm not spying on you." Mr. Herman leans forward with a conspiratorial grin. "I have elves for that."

"Ugh," Cheyenne says.

"Excellent dad joke." I high-five him.

"Thank you. Now what can I help you with?"

"Can you hand out these flyers to the parents? There's this holiday bonus at Once Upon, and it could really help bring in customers."

I show him the flyer and read along with him:

Merry Christmas, Shoppers! Santa might not have time to swing by the bookstore this year, but you do! Stop by Once Upon for all of your holiday reads. Ask for our most helpful elf, Shoshanna, and she'll find you the perfect story!

Cheyenne reads the flyer as well. "You're not an elf, Shoshanna. I mean, sure, you're close in height, but . . ."

"Rude," I say, then turn back to Mr. Herman. "And that's the second favor. Do you have any spare pairs of ears?"

"Say that three times fast," Cheyenne suggests.

"Spare pairs of ears," I try. "Spare pairs of ears. Spare pairs of—"

Mr. Herman cuts me off. "I do. Here, let me . . ." He digs into the prop Santa bag next to him, pulls out a pair, and passes them to me.

"Great!" Cheyenne says, and then glances around the mall again, as if trying to catch someone watching us. "So, we're done here, yeah? I love you and bye."

"Bye, Santa!" I say. "Thank you!"

Cheyenne and I hurry off the stage so the next kids can meet Santa. As we walk back to the Gap, I tell her, "Thank you. Seriously."

"You're welcome," she replies. "And I think we got out without Anna seeing us so, you know, crisis averted."

"Still lusting after her?" I ask.

She sighs. "More than lusting, I'm afraid. I really miss her. Not just kissing her but everything. I shouldn't have broken up with her. I was just . . ." She trails off, looking down at her black boots as we move through the crowds.

"You were just what?" I prod gently. I still don't really know why they broke up in the first place and just figured it was something I, the singleton, wouldn't understand.

Eventually, she responds, "I was scared she was going to break up with *me*."

Wait. What?

"I liked Anna, like *really liked* her." Cheyenne's voice hitches the tiniest bit, and I lean into her arm, head resting on her shoulder a short moment before the crowd jostles us forward. "But I was scared that the more I let her in, the more she'd see of me, and the less she'd like me. She'd see I wasn't really that great or something. I was scared that she'd break up with me, but like, at least if I ended the relationship I couldn't be rejected." She takes a quick breath. "Like if I quit things early I won't have a chance to fail at them."

My heart tugs for my best friend. I always assumed Cheyenne has a thousand hobbies because she enjoys flitting from one to the next—but maybe that's not it. Maybe she's scared of giving one thing her all and not having it reciprocated.

"Cheyenne," I say, a lump in my throat. I grab her hand to still us and let the shoppers part around us. "I don't know

Anna well enough to say for sure, but I'd bet there's at least an eighty percent chance the girl was not planning on breaking up with you. Because you, my friend, are fantastic. Smart and beautiful. Like, really beautiful. It's offensive, actually."

She laughs, eyes lighting up. "I know. And also I don't know. Self-confidence is a struggle, right?"

"The biggest struggle," I agree.

We smile at each other, but Cheyenne's smile quickly slips. She picks at one of her nails. "I just don't know what to do."

"Well, if you want to get back with Anna, and you did the breaking up, I think you've got to do the reconciling, you know? Make a gesture."

"Hmm." Cheyenne nods. "A gesture. Any ideas?"

"What does she like? Or what are some happy memories with her?" I ask. "Or—"

Cheyenne claps her hands together. "Oh! She's obsessed with the scones from Mel's Bakery, you know, at the shopping center next to the mall? They have these cheddar chive ones that are next level. I can call right now and have them delivered! Is that a good idea?"

"Baked goods are always a *great* idea."

"Yeah?" Her nervous smile breaks my heart and mends it right back up.

"Yeah." I wink. "Worked on y'all."

She nods, convinced. "Okay, I'm going to do it. Take my shot and all. Thanks, Shosh."

176

I step forward and give her a solid hug. "Anytime, Chey."

Jake walks into the break room the moment I put on my elf ears. His mouth twitches when he sees me. "Don't do it," I warn.

But his mouth twitches again, and he breaks into laughter. "Sorry." He holds up his hands. "I really tried."

I tilt my head. "Did you, though?" I put a hand on my hip. "C'mon. They can't look that ridiculous."

"They're elf ears, Shoshanna."

I huff and turn to face the cloudy and chipped break-room mirror. But it's positioned way too high above the sink, so I have to stand on my tiptoes to get a look, and then I can still only see the elf ears perched on top of my brown curls.

"Need a lift?" Jake offers.

My cheeks heat at that mental image: Jake's arms wrapped around my waist, lifting me up so his face presses against my back. Bryant in *Time Stands Still* is always lifting up Gracie when he's excited about something, launching her up into the air and spinning her around with glee. Once, he slid her back down his chest slowly, and then both breathing heavily, they kissed and—

"Shoshanna?"

"Hmm?" The top of my elf ears are probably bright red. "No, thank you. I'm sure they look fine. I'm heading back out to the floor. You coming?"

"Sure, was just getting a snack." Jake grabs a handful of almonds, and after I give him a look, he passes me a handful as well, and then we both walk out to the floor. "So," he says, popping an almond into his mouth. "What's up with the elf ears? We don't all have to dress up, do we? That wasn't in the job description."

"Just something I'm doing for fun!" I answer, as evasive as possible. A friendly competition is still a competition, and I don't need to let Jake in on my tactics.

A little girl trots up to us. Her mom trails behind, my flyer in her hand. "Shoshanna the Elf?" the girl asks, tugging on one of her pigtails.

Jiminy Cricket! It's working! Is this what Christmas joy feels like? Finally I understand what all of those gentiles are so excited about. Hopefully they don't mind me appropriating their culture to sell books.

I'm about to answer when I feel Jake step forward behind me. His voice is a low murmur, intrigued and amused. "How does she know your name?"

I ignore both the question and the pleasing chill that runs down my spine. And then I kneel down to meet the girl's eyes. "I *am* Shoshanna the Elf," I answer. "Thank you for the visit! Shall we take a look around? Would you like to hold my hand?"

I give her mom a quick *Don't worry, I'm not a creep* reassuring smile and then hold out my hand for the girl to grip before leading us all off toward the children's section.

"Do you mind if I see that flyer?" Jake asks the mom.

"Uh, sure," she says, and passes it over. I don't have time to wait for Jake's reaction, but I sneak a glance back as we walk and see an impressed look on his face.

"Nice one!" he calls out.

I feel a little glow of pride and chirp, "Thank you!" *Take that, stylized quiz.* Nothing a little personal touch and holiday cheer can't beat.

I help the girl and her mom find a selection of early reader books. One classic and two new releases. They head off to the register with my QR code in hand, and before I can straighten the shelves in front of me, another parent-and-child duo approach and ask if I'm Shoshanna the Elf.

It goes on like that for an hour straight with barely enough time for a quick bathroom break because Shoshanna the Elf needs to change her tampon, okay? I recommend picture books with glorious illustrations and middle-grade space adventures and magical chapter book box sets. One parent personally thanks me for the flyer and asks for adult recommendations next because they haven't been reading enough. It's amazing just how well my idea worked, and before I know it, I'm bouncing with bookselling adrenaline and knocking on Myra's door to ask for a new batch of codes.

"Come in!" she calls out.

When I step inside, I find her staring at her computer

screen, one hand massaging her temple, a single worry line creased across her forehead. I hesitate and consider coming back later, but then my nose gets all scratchy because apparently I'm allergic to elf ears, and I let out a giant sneeze. Myra startles and looks up at me. "Oh, right. Hi, Shoshanna."

"Hi!" I rub my nose with my cardigan sleeve. "May I have some more codes, please?"

Her eyes are distracted. It seems to take her a second too long to process my request, but eventually the words must click, and she says, "Sure. Well done." She rummages through her drawer and then hands me a new stack of codes.

"Thanks! So . . ." But Myra is already staring at her computer screen again, hand right back to temple-rubbing. "I'll just leave you to it, then. . . ."

I grab the stack of codes and exit her office, excited to get back to the customers flooding into the store. But then I notice something strange poking out above the young adult shelves. I walk over, round the corner, and—

"Seriously?" I ask.

"What?" Jake tugs on one of his elf ears with a grin. "I think I'm really pulling them off."

"You are not," I reply

Honestly, he's kind of pulling them off.

I cross my arms. "I'm going to win the competition."

His grin widens. "We'll see."

A new customer with a red flyer walks into the store, and

Jake the Elf gives me an audaciously charming wink before going to assist them.

"Darn you, Jake Kaplan," I mutter.

Looks like I'm going to need a new plan.

Chapter Twelve

Morning!" I say as I slide into the backseat of the car. The warmth greets me and immediately starts the work of defrosting my fingers. Honestly, how do people live up north? "Thank you for driving me again."

"You're welcome, mamaleh." Ms. Kaplan glances back at me with a smile. Her curls are particularly bouncy today. Very impressive spring factor. "Oh, you know what 'mama-leh' means, right?"

"I do. My mom speaks some Yiddish."

Mom offered to drive me to work today, but I could tell she was stressed about running late herself. And Mama was already out of the house to volunteer for a morning art class at the senior center. They've stopped fighting, at least that I can hear, but now the house is just silent. Like our family is on hiatus. I hope that therapy helps them. And I hope I can accept that I can't help them.

My stomach churns as I click my seat belt into place.

The thing is—I love my moms, a lot, and I want everything to be okay.

Ms. Kaplan pulls away from the curb and says, "I like that you've found a Jewish friend, Jakey. It's about time. Too many gentiles at that school of yours."

"Uh, Mom," Jake replies. "You're the one who moved us here from South Florida."

I snort. South Florida is also known as Jew Central—well, after New York.

"I couldn't deal with all that heat." She waves her hand. "And, oy! The humidity! It was relentless."

The ride to the mall zips by with Ms. Kaplan's chatter. She needs a new hobby and is thinking about watercolors. So of course I tell her about Mama's art. Jake brought a morning snack of cinnamon granola with dried banana and chili chocolate chips (absolutely to die for; like, I would lay down my body and become deceased in order to have another handful). And I discuss my favorite Time Stands Still fan theories when it turns out Ms. Kaplan loves the books as well. By the time we arrive at the mall and wave goodbye, my uneasy stomach has settled, and I'm even smiling.

"I really like your mom," I tell Jake as we walk. Now that we're out of the car, I notice that, for the first time ever, Jake isn't wearing flannel. Instead his shirt is this soft-looking jean material. I kind of want to touch it and find out just how soft, because as always, I'm a normal human person. He's also wearing my purple scarf around his neck, which gives me this absurdly toasty feeling inside so intense I have to look down at my boots to hide my heated cheeks.

"My mom likes you, too," Jake replies.

"Well, of course she does."

He laughs. "Of course?"

"I'm a nice Jewish girl. What's not to like?"

"Mm-hmm, nice." Jake knocks into my shoulder, then immediately reaches out to steady me, his hand pressed flat against my back for a quick moment before dropping away. "Kidding. You're a very nice Jewish girl, Shoshanna. It's indisputable."

I glow at his words. "Thanks." I do try to be a nice person, even if I messed up on that front a few times lately. I'm going to try to do more nice things and fewer impulsive, foot-in-mouth things in my future.

"How are, uh . . ." Jake scratches his neck, fingers dipped under the purple scarf. "How are things with your moms?"

I stuff my hands into the pockets of my dress. A year ago I ate dinner with my moms every night. A year ago the only fight in our house was over which movie to watch. A year ago we would take an annual skip day off of school and work to play mini golf and go bowling at Bonanza, a local entertainment center, and we'd also take last-minute weekend road trips to art fairs and flea markets outside of town.

But lately there isn't much of a *we*. And I don't know if there will be again. And all I can do is wait.

"Shoshanna?" Jake nudges.

We enter the mall through the Macy's entrance. Warm air blasts us, but I dig my hands into my coat pockets. "They're going to do therapy," I say. "After the holidays. So. We'll see."

There's a long silence, filled with nothing but our shoes clicking against the tile floor. We walk through the brightly lit cosmetics department. A woman attempts to spray us with perfume, but we both escape with a sharp left turn toward the main mall entrance. I'm a level-six perfume-spritz dodger.

"Therapy is good," Jake finally replies. "It's good they're trying. My dad . . . was never much of a trier."

Jake's dad.

I glance at Jake, at his tensed jaw and his hands fisted into his pockets. How have I never wondered about Jake's dad? "Do you want to talk about him?" I ask.

Jake clears his throat and looks down at his feet in this self-conscious way that makes me want to take his hand and hold it. I resist, because impulse control, but it's difficult. I imagine my hand would feel quite nice cupped in Jake Kaplan's.

He lets out a slow breath and then says, "My parents were married a long time ago." We walk into the main mall. Some of the stores are still shuttered, yet there's already a throng of early morning shoppers. "They loved each other, but Dad was immature, to say the least. He never took anything seriously, even once I was born. He'd get fired for coming in late for work and then blame it on having another hardass boss. He'd use the grocery money to buy pizza instead of fruits and vegetables. Nothing horrible . . . just exhausting. Mom hoped he'd mature, but it never happened."

"I'm sorry, Jake," I say. My shoulder presses into his because the mall corridors are already crowded with customers, definitely only because of that, and not because I feel angry for Jake, upset and hurt, and I want to comfort him in some small way. I can't feel the heat of his shoulder through my jacket, but I can imagine its warmth.

"Thanks." He breathes out the one word and then shrugs like it's no big deal, like he's talking about some random person not his dad. After a moment, he speaks again, his tone a little rushed, worried. "He's not a terrible person, you know? He made Mom pancakes every Saturday, and he made her laugh, and he loved her. But that wasn't enough. They divorced when I was four."

"Is he still, er, around?" I ask, not sure the right way to pose that question.

"Depends on your definition of 'around.'" Jake runs a hand through his curls. "He lives in New Jersey, takes care of my grandparents, and still can't seem to stick with a job longer than a few months. But he calls and sends birthday cards to me and some money to my mom, that kind of stuff. He's okay."

"Yeah, that's pretty good," I say, hoping my voice is bright when in reality there's a lump in my throat. Jake deserves more than birthday cards—and, well, now selfishly I can't help but wonder if that's what I'm facing. Is that what divorce means? Phone calls and cards?

Jake and I keep walking toward Once Upon, the crowds too thick and holiday music too loud now to continue our conversation. My fingers twist together. I don't want to be part of some checklist: *Water the plants, clean the bathroom, and call Shoshanna.* If my moms get divorced, it could happen so quickly. One of them could move out. And then slip away entirely.

"Just a little more glitter. . . ," Geraldine murmurs, brushing it across the boy's skin. He's delighted, as any child would be now that they look like a fantastical woodland creature, striped with green shadow and gold glitter.

"Impressive," I say.

"Very cool." The dad nods in agreement, only 60 percent distracted by his phone. He glances at me. "I just take this slip up to the register, right?" He holds my QR code and a couple of books in his free hand.

"Yep!" I reply. Since Jake stole my Shoshanna the Elf idea yesterday, I had to come up with a whole new plan. Thankfully, Geraldine had the morning off work and offered to provide face-painting services to customers, or, you know, the children of customers. Though Mr. Murillo's granddaughter did convince him to get a very distinguished pair of whiskers.

Geraldine adds a finishing touch of shimmer, and then the dad and his son head over to the register. For the first time in an hour we don't have another customer waiting, so Geraldine turns to me and says, "Guess who reached out to me last night."

The answer is obvious. I rock back on my heels and ask, "Lucille Tifton?"

"The one and only," Geraldine confirms. She's smiling, and her voice is upbeat, but a little bit of hurt still lingers in her eyes.

My stomach knots. I still can't believe I put my best friend through Internet torment hell. "And . . . what did Lucille Tifton say?"

"She apologized." Geraldine starts cleaning a makeup brush with a wipe. "She apologized *profusely*. Said sometimes she gets caught up in the Internet fury cycle, forgets how many fans she has and the power dynamic of it all. She regrets attacking me like that even if I had stolen her content."

"Oh," I say with a hint of relief. "That's good."

"Yeah." Geraldine finishes with one makeup brush and starts on another. Glitter is *everywhere*. Her fitted black sweater glimmers with a dusting of it. "So she's taking her attack video down and is going to post an apology video instead, and she's also . . ." A smile flits to Geraldine's lips. "She's also going to take me under her wing? Says she's been wanting to mentor new YouTubers for a while now, ones who don't have the resources she had access to. So she's going to help me with my videos and even send me a bunch of free products!"

"Oh my god!" I say. "That's amazing! That's like—exactly what you need to get started!"

"I know!" Geraldine agrees. "She'll probably send me more stuff in one box than I could afford to buy in a year. Being a beauty YouTuber is a rich person's game, but I'm going to carve out my own space."

"Damn right, you will." I glow with pride at my kickass best friend.

Geraldine grins at me. "I feel like I should almost thank you for posting my video without permission?"

"Please don't," I say quickly. "It'll just encourage me."

We both laugh as two little girls trot toward us with their dad in tow. Their eyes widen at Geraldine's case of cosmetics.

"Ooh," the older girl says.

"Ooooh," the younger girl says.

"Ooooooh," Geraldine says. "This is going to be a fun one."

She sets to work on the two girls, as I help their dad pick out books. After that, the flow of customers is constant. My stack of QR codes dwindles as quickly as Geraldine can apply eye shadow. And then Elliot shows up at eleven, breakfast sandwich in hand, and the two double-team the makeovers, raking in twice the amount of customers. Turns out Once Upon makeovers are much more exciting than standard blah Make You Up makeovers thanks to the help of copious amounts of glitter and colorful products turning kids into fairies, butterflies, and even a very impressive giraffe done by Elliot.

Eventually, my stack of QR codes run out, so I head to Myra's office. I glance down to find my dress shimmering and sparkling. I'll be showering off body glitter for the next week. I'm grateful things worked out for Geraldine. I'm really happy for her. But there's this catch at the back of my throat I'm trying to swallow away. Because things at home might not work out as easily.

I spy Jake on the way to Myra's office. He hasn't interrupted Mission Makeover because he's been busy with his own tactics. The store tablet is out once again, and there's a small semicircle of customers gathered around him. I watch as he sends one customer off to the history section and the next to romance. He's processing almost a customer a minute, which is way faster than the time it takes to turn a kid into a giraffe. *Darn you, technology.* What if Jake beats me *and* robots take over? Totally uncool.

Jake waves off a third customer and then turns toward Myra's office to find me in his path. He smiles as he walks over to me.

"Fancy running into you here," I say curtly, inspecting

a biography of George W. Bush like it's the most interesting thing in the world (spoiler: it's not).

"Good sales day?" Jake asks. His eyes are bright as they quickly inspect my dress. "Seems . . . *sparkly*."

"Very sparkly," I answer. "And yourself? Having a good sales day?"

He raises his crooked eyebrow. "Not shabby."

"You aren't going to make winning easy for me, are you?"

"Well, technically," Jake replies, stepping forward with a conspiratorial air, "winning won't be anything for you because I'm going to win."

I roll my eyes. "Oh my god."

"Oh my hashem," he corrects.

"Jew joke. Nice. Ten points to Gryffindor."

"Hmm." He tilts his head. "You think I'm a Gryffindor?"

"Well, you're not a Hufflepuff. And I thought you didn't read the books."

"Yes, well I've been known to occasionally watch those newfangled things called talking pictures."

I snort. "Newfangled?"

Jake laughs, and my skin gets all tingly, and we're grinning at each other like fools. And wow, he's so cute it physically hurts, like literally hurts my cheeks from smiling too much. The fact is, I've waded very deep into these crush waters, and there isn't a freaking lifeboat or plank of wood in sight.

I rock back on my heels and ask, "QR refill?"

Jake nods. "Yup. Myra will be proud."

"The most proudest."

"Do you get that excellent grammar from reading books?" he teases.

"Ha, ha," I reply as we walk to Myra's office. Her door is barely cracked, almost like she meant to shut it but didn't pull hard enough. I go to knock, but I still when I hear two voices. The tense conversation coming out of the office reminds me too much of my moms' fights at home. Jake gives me a funny look, but then the voices rise, and now he hears them too, Myra's voice and the deep timbre of someone else. Myra's husband, I think. He must be visiting. Are they fighting? Or . . .

"How much?" he asks.

"A couple thousand off, and even then it's only temporary. . . ."

"You think with the holiday bump it's possible?"

"It'd have to be a mighty bump." Jake and I exchange confused looks as Myra sighs. "If we triple sales before closing for Christmas, and if we get that grant money this summer, we could stay open. Otherwise, Once Upon is definitely closing its doors."

Wait. What?

Once Upon . . . closing?

Cold shock washes over me. The catch that's been in the back of my throat all day grows, and I choke back a soft cry.

That can't be right. Once Upon can't close. It's not possible. It's just not a thing that is within the realm of possibility. Once Upon isn't just a bookstore. It's a community. It's a home. It's *my* home, the thing I can depend on, no matter what, even if I'm having a bad day, even if Barbra breaks down, even if—even if my moms get divorced, Once Upon will be there for me.

It's always been there for me.

But now it might . . .

I'm light-headed as Myra's husband responds, "The store is packed. We could make it into the black and then figure out the rest in the New Year. Maybe there are other grants. It'll be all right, honey. No matter what you choose. I love you."

There's a long pause, but when Myra's voice comes out, it's soft and relaxed. "I love you too, Michael," she says. Through the cracked door I imagine his arm around her as they lean into each other, knowing that no matter what, they have each other.

"I need to head out soon," he says. "Fluffy will want to go on his walk."

At that, Jake and I quickly turn and dart to the break room. Once inside, the door slams shut behind us, and my heart races, not from the run but from the news, and I'm breathing hard, and there's this intense pressure pounding in my ears, and my head aches. "We weren't supposed to hear that," I manage to say.

"Definitely not. You okay?"

I look up and find Jake's concerned eyes, and I shake my head and whisper, *"No,"* and that small admittance cracks something open in me, and I start crying, not much, just a few frustrated tears, and then my body gets all shaky like I forgot to eat breakfast, and maybe I did forget to eat breakfast, but how does breakfast even matter when my moms might get divorced and Once Upon might close?

"I'm sorry," I say, voice hitching. "I'm sorry. Sorry."

"Hey, why are you—don't be—" Jake reaches out to me, his hands tentative on my shoulders, and I respond without thinking and move forward and burrow into his chest, getting warm tears all over his jean shirt, which for the record is just as freaking soft as it looks. There's a short moment of hesitation, and then Jake's arms wrap around my back, and he gives this deep exhale that vibrates through me, and he smells like maple syrup today, so sweet it makes me ache, and we stand like that for a long time before he speaks again, his mouth pressed against my hair. "There's nothing to be sorry about, Shoshanna. Things at home are tough, and I'm sure hearing Once Upon might close is really hard on top of that. I'd be upset too."

"Thank you," I murmur.

I allow myself to stay there in the warmth of his arms for three more seconds, counting them out, *one, two, three,* and then I slink away, back up against the counter, and hug myself tight. Jake stays where he is and tucks his hands in his pockets, his expression unreadable but skin lightly flushed. "You think . . ." He clears his throat. "You think that's what the bonus was about?"

"What do you mean?" I ask, but then the pieces click together. "Oh." The bonus wasn't about us or some fun holiday competition. It was to increase sales to keep the store open.

I'm not oblivious. I know bookstores aren't rolling in deep profit, but I assumed we were doing all right. How can we not be doing all right? This is Once Upon. It's an institution.

It can't just be over. We can't just let it go.

My shoulders stiffen as determination edges into my voice. "We have to do something," I tell Jake. "Save the store. Keep it open. We'll . . ." I begin to pace around the room. "We'll tell our coworkers what we overheard, and we'll get everyone to help. Full-force bookselling. We'll make a tactical plan, like it's a freaking war, but a war for literacy and cute journals with cats on the cover, and we'll—"

"Shoshanna," Jake cuts me off.

"What?" I glance at him. His crooked eyebrow is raised, and my excitement plummets back down. "Right," I say. "Okay. Maybe don't tell our coworkers a conversation we weren't supposed to hear. Probably not a mature move."

I can see him forcing back a smile. "Probably not."

"But I can't just sit here!" I say, pacing again. "I can't do nothing! Okay, what if . . . Okay, I know this is out there . . .

but what if we talked to Myra? Told her we overheard her conversation and want to help?"

"Yeah." Jake scratches his jaw in thought. "That could work."

"Totally. It could totally work." I press my hands together. "It has to work. We can't let Once Upon become Ever After."

"That's an impressive on-the-spot pun," Jake says.

"I know." I nod, voice solemn. "But praise me later. We have a store to save."

Chapter Thirteen

There's a clock in Myra's office, a novelty item from the Time Stands Still movies. In the movies it sits on Sherriff Jacobs's wall, hands frozen in place at 2:47. Until the last movie, when the town has been saved and is thrust back into movement, and the film closes on a shot of the minute hand ticking to 2:48.

That novelty clock is ticking now as I wait for Myra to respond. One tick every second. I never noticed it before, but now the *tick, tick, tick* makes my hands itch for a baseball bat.

I told Jake I wanted to do this alone, so he's back on the floor, and it's just Myra and me. I filled her in on what we overheard, and I pleaded the case and said we want to help. Now it's silent, and Myra is sitting at her desk, silent, as the clock *tick, tick, tick*s. Finally, she shifts forward in her chair and sighs. "I didn't want you to hear that conversation."

"I know," I say. "And I'm sorry. But we did hear it, and we want to help. Will you let us help? We can make that profit you need. I know it."

"It's not only about the money." Myra slips off her glasses so they hang on their pink crocheted chain around her neck. "This store takes a lot of work, Shoshanna. Even when we're doing well, it's a marathon, and I don't know if I want to keep running."

"Please," I say. "Just give us a chance! We can turn things around. I can get everyone to help."

"You can't tell *anyone* else what you overheard. I don't want to ruin the holidays. I haven't decided if we're closing, but if we are, I'll tell them after the New Year. We'll stay open for at least a few months so everyone has time to find new employment."

"I won't tell anyone," I promise. "I can just say that we're . . . throwing a party! We can invite all of our customers and the holiday crowd. It'll be this giant, festive celebration, and we'll make a ton of profit. And if you still choose to close the store, at least the party will be something incredible to remember it by."

Myra gives me a long, hard look. I swear the clock ticks even louder. But eventually she nods and says, "Your budget is one hundred dollars. Not a penny more. Got it?"

"Yes! Definitely!"

"And I'm making no promises. Understood?"

"Yes!" I mentally pump my fist into the air and dance around the room. "I totally and completely understand."

* * *

From: *Myra@OnceUpon.com*

To: *Employees@OnceUpon.com*

12:34 p.m.

> I have given Shoshanna permission to throw a **festive celebration** tomorrow before we close on Christmas Eve. Participation is completely—**completely**—voluntary. If you would like to take part, she is holding a meeting in the break room at 1:00 p.m.
>
> —Myra

From: *Shoshanna@OnceUpon.com*

To: *Employees@OnceUpon.com*

> Which one of you nerds has a whiteboard?
>
> —Shoshanna

From: *SophieAnne@OnceUpon.com*

To: *Employees@OnceUpon.com*

> I have one in my car.

From: *Shoshanna@OnceUpon.com*

To: *Employees@OnceUpon.com*

> Really??

From: *Arjun@OnceUpon.com*

To: *Employees@OnceUpon.com*

> TAG ME OUT

From: *Myra@OnceUpon.com*

To: *Employees@OnceUpon.com*

    Tag us all out. Now.

From: *Shoshanna@OnceUpon.com*

To: *SophieAnne@OnceUpon.com*

    Please bring your whiteboard to the meeting!

From: *SophieAnne@OnceUpon.com*

To: *Shoshanna@OnceUpon.com*

    Fine.

I stack five boxes of hardcovers, three on bottom and two on top, then climb up and stand on them. Huh. So this is what it's like to look down on people instead of up at them. It's a whole new world. Since it's the busiest shopping day of the year, almost our entire staff is working. A few people are left on registers to keep the store afloat and because they don't care about our *festive celebration*, but the majority of the Once Upon staff is gathered before me in the stock room, even Arjun, who e-mail-screamed TAG ME OUT.

My coworkers are assembled before me like a superhero team, except not at all like a superhero team. Everyone is scrolling on their phones, tapping their feet, picking lint off of their sweaters, and looking all-around restless. Keeping staff off of the floor defeats the purpose of saving the store, so I need to get this done quickly. I tug on my necklace and glance at Jake, who's on my left and not standing on a throne of boxes. He gives me a reassuring nod, and I straighten my shoulders with a little more confidence.

"Okay." I clap my hands together. "Thank you, everyone, for being here."

"You're welcome!" Geraldine says.

"She doesn't even go here," Arjun replies.

Wait. Did Arjun just make a *Mean Girls* reference?

"Why are we here, exactly?" Tanya asks, perennial mug of tea in hand.

"Why *are* we here?" Daniel steps forward as he straightens his glasses. *Daniel*, who considers this store a home as much as I do. My heart squeezes. God, it hurts like hell that I can't tell him that Once Upon might close.

My throat tightens, and I'm worried I might start crying on my throne of boxes. I'm tempted to turn this meeting over to Jake, but I owe it to myself, to Myra, to the store, to get through this. I take a breath and force my voice to be bright. "We are here because we're going to throw a party! A great party. A festive party. Um, a—"

The break room door bangs open, and Sophie-Anne sidles in with a massive whiteboard, her skirt trailing behind her like a gauzy black wedding-dress train. The crowd parts for her and the whiteboard, but I still hear the *ouch* of a banged elbow.

"Why do you have a whiteboard in your car?" Daniel asks.

"I tutor kids," Sophie-Anne replies.

"You . . . tutor?" he asks.

"Yes," she replies, breaking through the crowd to where I'm standing.

"You tutor . . . children?" I clarify.

Sophie-Anne ignores my question as she props the whiteboard up against the wall. "Why do we even need this?"

"For party planning!" I say.

"And we're throwing a party . . . tomorrow?" Tanya asks, her brow creased. Tanya's husband works one of those full-time nine-to-five jobs with benefits, but with two young boys at home to support, I'm sure Tanya doesn't work at Once Upon for the fun of it and to supply her coworkers with emergency tampons. I'm sure she needs this paycheck. She needs this store.

My eyes sweep across the room and take in every familiar face, and it fully hits me then. It's not just Once Upon, my happy place, on the line here—it's on the line for all of us. I can't imagine a world without Once Upon, without its endless stacks of curated books, without Mr. and Mrs. Murillo hosting story time for kids curled up in beanbag chairs and Ms. Serrano puttering around with her cup of coffee, handing out recommendations left and right like she's an employee, without Daniel and Tanya and even Arjun and Sophie-Anne.

Because this place isn't just a store. It's a home. And I'm going to do my darn-all to keep it.

"Yes," I say, drawing in a breath. "We're throwing a party tomorrow!" I step down off my throne and up to Sophie-Anne. "Marker me," I tell her, holding out my hand.

She slaps an Expo marker into my palm. Hard. *Ouch.* But good. I uncap the marker and turn to the whiteboard. Okay, brainstorming. I'm brainstorming a party. I have about ten seconds before I lose the attention of these employees, and it's hard to think when the store Christmas music is on full blast today. If that cheery reindeer song plays one more freaking time, I swear I'll fully empathize with the Grinch, and—wait!

"That's it!" I say.

"What's it?" Daniel asks.

I turn back to everyone and shout, "The Grinch who Stole Bookmas!" The plan forms so quickly in my head it must be a Christmas miracle. *Yes.* This is going to be epic! Some of my coworkers are looking at me with concern, perhaps worried the holiday retail rush has pushed me past the edge of sanity, but I ignore those alarmed looks and say, "We'll tell everyone the Grinch stole Bookmas! He ran around and stole every-one's favorite books and hid them all over the mall. It'll be like a scavenger hunt!"

Tanya raises her hand. "How does that get people into the store, though?"

I nod. "Right. Good question. Well, we won't hide actual books. We can print out vouchers for the books, hide those, and then people can redeem them for the actual book at the store. And it won't just be the scavenger hunt—we'll have snacks and drinks, and maybe we can get some stores to donate gift certificates for raffles, and . . ."

"Ooh!" Geraldine jumps up and down. "Elliot and I can do more face paint."

"Yes, perfect!" I say. "And maybe I can get Santa to come—I know him!"

Jake narrows his eyes. "You *know* Santa?"

"Don't worry about it." I wave him off and turn back to the whiteboard. "Okay, people. More ideas! Hit me!"

Twenty minutes later, we have a whiteboard of ideas and a full plan of action for the party. Most employees have returned to the store floor, but Daniel is still back here, and Sophie-Anne and Arjun are as well. They're both drawing in the corner of the whiteboard. I guess it is *her* whiteboard.

I let out a giant yawn as Daniel walks over to me. It's going to be a twenty-four-hour marathon of tireless effort and little sleep, and I'm already exhausted, but this has to work. We have to save the store. And I think with this plan, it's possible.

"You okay there?" Daniel asks.

"Yeah." I muster a smile. "Just tired." *And completely over-*

whelmed at the thought of my favorite place in the world closing forever and racked with guilt that I can't tell you about it, but other than that, yep, totally and completely fine.

"Hmm," Daniel says. Then he turns and calls out, "Hey, Arjun!"

"What?" Arjun whines. He's drawing what looks like a duck exorcism.

Sophie-Anne glances down at his creation and says, "Aw! Cute, babe! Your craft is really improving."

He beams up at her. "Thanks, hon!"

Daniel and I exchange a look but say nothing. Then Daniel asks, "Arjun, can you come over here?"

Arjun sighs but caps his marker and walks over to us. Daniel slips him a ten-dollar bill from his wallet. "One peppermint mocha with extra cream and syrup, and then one more extra pump of syrup just to be safe."

"Sophie-Anne and I don't like coffee," Arjun responds. "We like whole-grass wheat juice."

"And vodka," Sophie-Anne chimes in.

"And vodka," Arjun agrees.

"The order isn't for you." There's a long, stretched-out silence until Daniel gets the hint and digs another bill out of his wallet. "Here, get your grass juice or whatever."

Arjun takes the money. "Okay."

As he leaves, I turn to Daniel with a grin. "You really don't have to do that."

"Hey." Daniel raises an eyebrow. "How do you know that peppermint mocha is for you?"

"Because your mother is a dentist and would murder you for drinking something that cavity-inducing."

"Fair enough." Daniel laughs, then removes his glasses and cleans them with the bottom of his T-shirt. I notice a slight tremor in his hand. My muscles tense at the sight of it. "Shoshanna . . ." He looks up at me. "Are you sure this is just a party? Is something else going on here? You can tell me, you know."

His eyes lock with mine, and my pulse races.

What if the store closes? Will I see Daniel again? Will he get a job at his college campus bookstore with the notoriously terrible predilection for dead white male authors? Will I ever again sit on the floor with Lola and him and eat our way through an entire bag of Hi-Chew candies? Will we ever have another hourlong conversation about the merits of superfluous food porn in high fantasy novels? The thought of never seeing Daniel again, the thought of that potential loss, hits me hard, and I take a sharp breath.

I can see his nerves—I can *feel* them—from his tense jaw to his tapping foot. I want to tell him the truth, but I can't. It's not my secret to share, and I've learned my lesson about overstepping boundaries. So instead I stuff my hands into my pockets and force a smile. "Yeah, everything is great! Just a party to celebrate the holidays. It'll be fun!"

"Right." Daniel eyes me. "Okay, then."

His foot taps harder.

"Is this about to get X-rated?" Geraldine asks.

We're in the food court. Geraldine is done with face painting and about to start her shift at Bo's Burritos, and I'm about to ask her manager, Vincent, to "sponsor" the Bookmas event by donating a gift certificate. But it's hard to focus when in a corner booth Cheyenne and Anna are in the midst of a hardcore make-out session. Like fully wrapped around each other, fused into one being, tonsil-hockey hardcore. Looks like those cheddar chive scones worked wonders.

"I guess they made up," I observe.

"Yup," Geraldine agrees. "Looks that way."

"We should probably stop watching."

"Yeah." Geraldine tilts her head. "But the athleticism is extraordinary."

"Masterful breathing technique. Truly."

Geraldine laughs. "Okay, this is getting creepy."

"Definitely weird," I agree. "Let's, um, let's go talk to your manager."

Geraldine clocks into work, and I ask to chat with Vincent. Ten minutes later I've convinced him that sponsoring our Bookmas event is truly a once-in-a-lifetime branding opportunity for Bo's Burritos that could cement the moral foundation of the company forever, and there's a twenty-five-dollar gift certificate in my hand as I walk back into the food court. Cheyenne and Anna have pulled apart and are now using their mouths to instead talk and giggle.

"Hey, y'all!" I walk over to them with a wave. "Chey, is your dad working today?"

Cheyenne puts her face in her hands. "Not until later."

"Hey, Shoshanna!" Anna greets me. Her short hair is mussed from the make-out, and her cheeks are reddened. She picks up a bottle of water and sips.

"Hi, hi!" I slide into the booth next to Cheyenne. "Nice to see y'all have . . . reacquainted."

Anna laughs. "That's a word for it." They both look at each other with smiles warmer than Georgia in July. Ugh. The freaking cuteness. "What's that?" Anna asks me, gesturing to the gift certificate in my hand.

I tell them both about the Bookmas party but not about the store being in danger. Myra probably wouldn't mind if I told my best friends, but I can't chance the secret slipping. Anna says she can probably get Nordstrom to "sponsor" as well, and then I tell Cheyenne, "I might also need another favor from Santa."

She glances at Anna and then at me and then shakes her head with a laugh. "You sure are lucky I'm in such a good mood today."

I grin. "Yes, I am."

* * *

The rest of the day rushes by in a flurry of bookselling and event preparation. Daniel and I make a list of places to hide all of the book vouchers so we can write the hints on the flyers, and it turns out Sophie-Anne is not only a talented artist at disturbing content but also a talented artist at wholesome holiday fun, so she designs the flyer. We then e-mail it to our customers and also print it to hand out around the mall. I've secured gift certificates from Bo's Burritos, Nordstrom, Make You Up, and the Dead Sea lotion stall, after a very flustered interaction with a guy who must model for *GQ* on his off hours, and Santa promised to show up tomorrow at two p.m. sharp to kick off the festivities.

And now it's eight in the evening, and I'm no longer at Once Upon. Instead, I'm outside, standing on the stoop of Jake Kaplan's house with Daniel and Lola, cold wind biting at my skin as I ring the doorbell. We went to pick up Daniel's cookie cutters after work, while Jake and his mom took Myra's stipend to buy baking supplies.

Jake's house is one story and painted pale yellow with light blue shutters. There's a little rock garden out front with a sign that says JUST ROLL WITH IT. A single glowing light shines over the front door. The whole picture is the definition of "homey," and I want to see the rest of it. The kitchen with all of Jake's spices. The living room with his mom's decorations. Jake's bedroom . . . to see what he hangs on his walls and what tchotchkes line his shelves, to see the color of his comforter. I bet he has a really worn-in pillow, perfectly fit to the shape of his head.

Oy. This crush has become a very big and unwieldy thing.

Jake opens the door, and Daniel announces, "I've got trees, I've got Santas, and I've got reindeers."

"Good." Jake grins. "Because I only have dreidels and menorahs."

"I have no cookie cutters, but I have excellent taste buds ready to taste test any and all cookie batter and frosting!" Lola says.

"Me too!" I add.

"Awesome." As Jake smiles, he seems to angle his head so he's smiling right at me in particular, and his eyes are warm and a little sleepy, and his hair is all rumpled like he maybe took a five-minute nap after the grocery store. And instead of his flannel or jean shirt, he's wearing an apron over a plain white T-shirt, and apparently Jake Kaplan has muscles, like biceps-with-a-capital-"B" muscles, which you probably get from bussing tables and kneading dough, and my heart is thumping so loud against my rib cage I bet the neighbors can hear it, and oh my hashem, I am way too into this guy.

Jake holds the door open wider. "Come on in, y'all."

Yes. Yes, I will.

We all file into the house, and I may or may not inhale as I slide by Jake. Cinnamon. And something deeper. Cloves? What do cloves smell like?

"Hi, Shoshanna!" Ms. Kaplan greets me. "And you two must be Daniel and Lola! Welcome!" A headband pushes back her curls, and an apron hangs over her clothes. I smile as I read the words stitched into the apron: ASK PERMISSION BEFORE YOU KISS THE COOK. "Are we ready for some baking?"

"Mom is helping," Jake says. "She . . . insisted."

"You could sound a little more grateful, Jakey."

"Yeah, Jakey," I add, nudging his shoulder. "You could sound a little more grateful."

He nudges my shoulder back as Ms. Kaplan grins at me. "I knew I liked you, mamaleh. That's a cute dress."

Today I'm wearing a yellow affair printed with different book covers. I curtsy. "Thanks!"

Ms. Kaplan puts on a Temptations station, and we all get to work. Jake tells us we're making cinnamon snap cookies and dark chocolate candy-cane cookies, and before I know it, we're all measuring and mixing and scooping while singing along to "My Girl," and it's warm in the kitchen but not too warm, and it smells like peppermint, and I'm smiling and happy, but I also feel this tiny ache because this is what the holidays should be like, this is what my holidays used to be like, minus the Christmas cookie cutters, and I hope more than anything therapy will work, and soon my family will be the one singing in the kitchen.

When the song changes, I notice Jake standing still in front of the corner counter. His expression is tense as he dips a spoon into a bowl, takes a taste, and shakes his head. I walk over to him and say, "Pretty intense vibe you've got going on."

Jake glances at me, and my pulse jumps. Dear lord, he's cute up close. "Just can't get the recipe right," he tells me. "It's missing something."

"The cookies don't have to be perfect."

"I know. But I like making perfect cookies." He shoots me a quick grin and nudges my shoulder, and I'm standing in Jake Kaplan's kitchen, and he's grinning at me and nudging my shoulder. "Plus," he continues, lowering his voice to a whisper, "maybe a perfect cookie will save the store."

I swallow hard as his eyes stay focused on mine. Once Upon might just be a job for Jake, but it's so much more than that for me, and it feels indescribably nice that he wants to make a perfect cookie to save the place I love so much.

I duck my head down, then scoot forward to the counter. "Can I help?"

"Yeah, can you taste it?" he asks.

Oh, I can definitely taste it.

However, Jake's mind is *not* next to mine in the gutter. He scoops out cookie dough with a fresh spoon and hands it to me. I take a bite, and there's sugar and cinnamon, so of course it's delicious, but Jake is eyeing me like he's waiting for some sort of culinary breakthrough. "Um . . ." I close my eyes and really concentrate on the flavor, channeling *The*

Great British Baking Show. Come on, Mary Berry. Speak to me. When I open my eyes again, Jake's steady gaze is still on me. My skin tingles as I suggest, "Salt?"

He stills for a moment, and I hold my breath, expecting him to knock down the suggestion, but then he smacks his head. "Wow. I forgot salt. How did I forget salt?"

I grin. "Ten hours of bookselling during the holiday season can do that to anyone. Don't beat yourself up about it."

"Right, thanks," Jake says, and grabs a container of kosher salt from the pantry. He adds it bit by bit, mixing it in with care. Watching Jake bake might be the most relaxing thing I've ever witnessed. Maybe *he* should be a YouTuber, a channel called "Jake Bakes," but then everyone might think that channel is about smoking weed . . . though I bet stoners would actually love watching Jake bake cookies.

"Shoshanna," someone suddenly whispers behind me. I jump at least a foot in the air. Okay, I jump, like, half an inch in the air. Then I turn to find Lola, and she's grinning real hard and raising her eyebrows, which I've just noticed are also pink to match her hair. "You were staring, *a lot*, just FYI."

My neck heats, and I glance around to make sure no one heard her or saw me *Fatal Attraction*–staring, not that I've ever watched *Fatal Attraction*, but I've got to assume there's creepy staring at some point in that movie. Thankfully Jake is focused on his salt, and Daniel and Ms. Kaplan are rolling out the first batch of cookie dough. I grab Lola's hand and pull her into the living room. "Was it obvious?" I ask.

She straightens the Oxford collar of her dress. "Er, kind of. But hey. Nothing to be embarrassed about. He's cute, and he *bakes*. You should go for it."

I *should* go for it. But I don't really know how to go for it. And what if he doesn't want to go for it? What if I'm just the funny, different girl to him? And suddenly I understand how nervous Cheyenne felt because it's really freaking nerve-racking to like someone, really like someone, and not know if they return the feeling.

"Maybe," I say.

"Definitely," Lola says.

We return to the kitchen, and for the next two hours, it's baking and Temptations singing and cookie frosting, and even though I'm exhausted and nervous as heck about tomorrow, I'm also happy and smiling more than I have in ages.

Finally, the finish line is in sight. We frost the last batch of cookies, while Daniel washes the dishes. The mug of spiced apple cider Ms. Kaplan served an hour ago hits my bladder with a sudden vengeance, and I excuse myself to use the restroom. After washing my hands, I leave the bathroom to head back to the kitchen, but that's when I notice a cracked door with soft lamplight filtering into the hallway. I stop in my tracks and stare.

Don't snoop. Don't snoop. Don't be a snooping snooper.

I take a step toward the cracked door and then another.

Shoshanna, go back to the kitchen. Frost cookies.

I nudge open the door with the slightest bump of my elbow.

This is disrespectful, immature, and—

I peek inside the room. And, yes, it's Jake Kaplan's bedroom.

His bedside lamp is on, bathing the room in soft yellow light. His bed is made, barely, a rumpled navy comforter pulled up over his pillows. The floor is clean, mostly, with a few pairs of shoes and socks tumbling out of the closet. His desk—his desk looks like mine. It's consumed by papers and pens, a level five, mad-scientist disaster zone of creative glory. My feet take control and step into the room. I walk over to the desk and find a dozen scattered recipes, ideas for everything from the cinnamon snap cookies we made tonight to Bubbie's shepherd's pie to deconstructed babka. His handwriting is *terrible*. Absolutely awful. Scratchy and almost illegible.

I love it.

I want to steal of scrap of it and hide it in my wallet.

"Toilet's in the other room," a voice says.

"SORRY!" I both scream and jump, then squeak, then turn to Jake as I slap my hands over my extremely red cheeks. "Sorry. I'm terrible."

He grins. And is it just me, or does Jake's cute grin

become a *sexy* grin when it shows up inside his bedroom? He takes a couple of steps toward me, and I consider dying, or flinging myself onto his bed, or running from the room and never returning to the mall again. But before I can do any of that, he says, "You're fine. I'd be curious too."

"Are you saying you'd sneak into *my* bedroom?"

"Better keep your windows locked."

We both stare at each other for a long beat.

"That was—" I say.

"Creepy—" Jake says.

"Seriously creepy."

"Insanely creepy. I don't know why I said that."

We both laugh. Jake rubs a hand over his jaw, then leans back and throws open his arms, casting his gaze around the room. "So. What do you think of the place?"

"It's cute," I say.

"Cute?"

"I like the recipes. And the elephant."

Jake groans. "Was hoping you wouldn't see that."

I almost didn't. But in the corner of the bed there's a yellow stuffed animal elephant. It looks well-worn and loved, like it's been living in that bed for years. "Does he have a name?" I ask.

"*Her* name is Elle."

"Elle." I nod. "Elle the elephant. Creative."

"I was four. My dad, uh." Jake clears his throat and starts

moving around the room. "My dad got her for me the year he moved out. Okay . . . actually, that's really embarrassing, isn't it?" He crouches down to organize the shoes spilling out of his closet and is basically muttering now. "Note to self: Don't keep the stuffed animal from your dad on your bed when a pretty girl is coming over."

Did Jake just say I'm—

I step forward. "Did you just say I'm—"

"Jake!" Ms. Kaplan screams from the kitchen. "We need another batch of frosting!"

Jake stands back up and shouts, "Coming!"

"Great lung capacity in the family," I observe.

He looks at me with this kind of funny smile that makes me feel like I've been pumped full of caffeine and chocolate and maybe even a couple of narcotics, and then he shakes his head, and then he says, "Shoshanna, you're—"

"Jacob Mordechai Kaplan!" his mom shouts again.

"I said I'm coming!" he screams back. Then softer to me, "Come on, frosting emergency."

I'm what? I'm what? I want to ask, but I follow him out of the room and back into the kitchen, and he whips up a final batch of frosting, and we finish the cookies, and then it's midnight, and we're all yawning, and Ms. Kaplan has changed into her pj's and says, "I love you all, but get out of my house."

I file outside with Daniel and Lola. Jake stands in the

doorway as we walk to the car, and when I glance back, I see a bit of frosting on his cheek, and I want to wipe that frosting off, and then maybe kiss that cheek, and maybe Lola is right, maybe I should go for it.

And maybe tomorrow I will.

"You're up late," I tell Mama.

We're *both* up late. It's past midnight, and Daniel just dropped me off at home. But when I walked into our house, I noticed the back porch light was on and went to investigate. I lean against the doorframe now, head heavy and thoughts drowsy after the long day. "Waiting up for me?" I ask.

"Maybe." Mama turns away from her easel to look at me. She taps her watch with a smile. "You did say before midnight, and it's five after, missy."

"I'm such a rebel."

"Sure you are." She winks and then flicks her gaze back to the easel. Her blond hair falls smooth against her back, like she just combed it. "What do you think? Does it need to be lighter?" I walk farther into the screened-in porch. Two space heaters whir with concentrated effort, holding the cold at bay. Mama twirls a paintbrush as she gazes at her beautiful mountain landscape, a crystalline lake shining at the bottom.

I step up to the painting and inspect closely. Mama's body radiates heat, and my thoughts feel even drowsier now, dreamlike, spun up in cotton. "A little lighter," I say. "Maybe some pinks in the sky there."

"Good idea." She nods and then swipes her brush into her paints. "Yes, right here." She blends in the color with a few simple strokes. "Thanks, darling."

"Sure." I crack a tiny yawn and stretch one arm in front of my chest. "No problem."

She adds one more swirl of color as she asks, "So tell me again, why were you out baking cookies at midnight? You said there's a holiday party?" She finishes with the adjustment, then puts down her brush and motions to our rocking chairs, a pair of wicker ones with a table and potted plant between them. "Come on. Sit with me a little." Mama cinches her knitted cardigan as she takes a seat.

It's late, real late, and I'm tired, real tired, but that means my mind is too sleepy to make decisions on its own. Besides, it feels nice here out on the porch with the space heaters and Mama's soothing voice. I sit down next to her and rock a few times, eyes half closed as I tell her about the holiday party— and then—and then I tell her why we're throwing the holiday party. There's a catch in my throat as I reveal Once Upon might close, as I see the surprise, then the empathy in Mama's eyes. I know the secret will be safe with her, and I need to talk about it with someone.

Being out here on the porch tonight feels like a bubble, safe and tranquil, not unlike the world of *Time Stands Still*.

Yes, the town was under a curse, but there was also something comforting about being frozen in time, about living in the before.

We're still in the before now. Mom and Mama are still married. Once Upon is still open. I like things as they are. I don't want them to change. I'm not ready to live in the after.

"I love Once Upon," I say. My voice wobbles, my fingers twist together—it's not the thought of Once Upon closing that knots my stomach the tightest. "I don't want to lose it."

I don't want to lose our family.

Moisture pricks at my eyes as I yank on the sleeves of my cardigan. "Sorry." I shake my head. "I'm being too sensitive."

"Too sensitive?" Mama asks, confusion etched into her tone.

"Yeah. Like I've been too emotional about stuff." I wave my hand, try to make my voice light. "Crying too easily. Too sensitive. I've been all over the place lately."

"Shoshanna," Mama says. Her eyes lock with mine, and her gaze is warm, protective, like a heavy blanket on a cold night. "I love that you're sensitive. It means you *care*. That's a good thing."

I swallow hard. "Yeah?"

She nods, and I realize there are a few tears in her eyes, and I laugh because you don't have to be related by blood to inherit something from your parent. "*Yeah,*" Mama says. "It's like a superpower, caring about people the way you do. Look at Geraldine and Cheyenne. Not everyone has friendships like that because you need to nurture relationships, care for your friends as deeply as you care for yourself, and that's what you do, and I know they do the same for you."

"I do have great friends." I pause. My gaze flicks to my feet as I try to form the next words without crying, even though we just established crying is okay. I take a shaky breath and then admit, "I've been worried about you and Mom. Not knowing what will happen. It's scary."

"I'm sorry, sweetheart." Mama glances out the window. In the moonlight, we can just see the silhouettes of our bare trees. "It upsets me, too. But I promise we'll figure something out."

"Something" is a very vague word.

"You know," Mama continues, her tone more relaxed. "This might come as a surprise, but your mom and I aren't perfect. No one is."

I gasp and hold a hand to my chest. "Are you saying I, the magnificent Shoshanna Greenberg, daughter of yours, light of your life, am not perfect?"

She laughs, eyes brightening. "Afraid I am. I hope you can move past this great insult."

"Only time will tell."

Mama grins. "C'mon." She stands, takes my hand, and tugs me out of my chair.

It really is nice out here, snug as the heaters battle the

cold air pressing in against the screens. We finish Mama's painting together, cozy and content. And it's true. Only time will tell. And there's no stopping time. The minutes slip by into tomorrow, and we begin to live in the after.

Chapter Fourteen

I'll do it!" I offer.

"No problem!" I say.

"On it!" I call out.

For the next few hours I volunteer for every task, whether it's as menial as re-alphabetizing our shelves or as gross as changing the liners in our trash cans (freaking *ew* to the person who dumped out an entire congealed bowl of Panera's broccoli cheddar soup). I do anything possible to help the store and prepare for the Bookmas event—because the second I stop moving, a panicked feeling vibrates through me, growing more and more wild until I find a new task to fling myself at.

So when Daniel group-texts and asks who has time to hide the book vouchers, I volunteer immediately. And then my phone chimes with another text, one from Jake: I'll go with her

"If that's okay with you," Jake adds, and I spin to find him behind me, eyebrow arched and *nine* books stacked in the crook of his arm. He's getting, *aggressively*, good at that.

Mom drove me into work today, so I've barely seen Jake this morning. You might say my eyes now hungrily sweep over him, taking in everything from his plaid shirt, deep purple and black today, to the curve of his jaw to his scuffed boots. He smells like buttered croissants.

With flushed cheeks, I finally reply, "Of course it's okay with me."

He smiles. "Good."

I shrug and smile back. "Good."

Ten minutes later, the vouchers and some extra flyers are stuffed into my tote bag, and we venture out into the mall. It's creeping toward noon, and the place seems to have hit full capacity, like Black Friday–level crowds.

Our e-mail blast was a success. A ton of our regular customers said they'd stop by for the party. Ms. Serrano said she wouldn't miss it for the world, and the Murillos offered to host a holiday-themed story hour. I'm just praying we can rope in all of these other shoppers, get them to participate and buy books. This event could be the tipping point between Once Upon staying open or closing.

Our flyers list all the book titles with hints about where they might be hidden, but we've only picked store locations, not specific hiding spots. Our first stop: the bedding section of Macy's for our *Goodnight Moon* voucher. As we walk, the crowd jostles us like balls inside a pinball machine. I ask

Jake, "How are the cookies this morning?"

"The cookies are—" Jake disappears momentarily as a man who must be at least six feet five sidles between us. I'm not above admitting my pulse skips at Jake's seconds-long absence, then skips again upon his reappearance. I like Jake at my side. I like being able to look at him out of the corner of my eye while pretending to look at store marquees and holiday decorations. Six-foot-five-inch men can stay the heck away, thanks very much. "—frosted and waiting patiently in the stock room," Jake finally finishes. "That place is like a freezer."

"Artic-level cold," I agree. "Thank you for helping. And thank your mom, too. It was a lot of work, and you guys didn't have to do it."

Jake shrugs, then stuffs his hands into his pockets. "We wanted to help."

"I don't want to distract you from winning the bonus." I nudge him and tease. "I know you're in need of all the help you can get if you want to beat me."

"Ha, ha." He eyes me with a smile. "Are you so confident you'll win?"

"Kind of." I shrug. "I don't know. Now I'd feel weird about keeping the money if I do win. Though I doubt it's enough money to keep the store open. But at the same time, it's a lot of money. I guess money is weird that way. It can mean so much and so little depending on the circumstance. I *could* really use it. . . ." I trail off.

"To fix Barbra?" Jake asks.

"Yup." I sigh. "Poor girl is gathering dust in the driveway. I swear this morning I saw a cobweb claiming territory on one of her tires." We make it into Macy's and take an escalator down to the home goods section. "What do you need the bonus money for? If you don't mind me asking."

"I don't mind." Jake runs a hand through his hair as we descend. He's on the step before mine, and I may or may not be creeping on the back of his neck, which is apparently on my list of top-five places to creep on Jake. I clench my hands tightly around my tote bag so they don't get any ideas. "I'm going to use it to help buy a plane ticket," he answers.

"Oh," I respond as we step off of the escalator. I'm not sure what I expected, but I feel some level of surprise. "To see your dad?"

Jake shakes his head. "Nah, to send Mom to see her mom, my bubbie. She lives out in California. Money is tight, and the fare is expensive. Mom hasn't seen her in two years."

Jesus.

Or Moses. Whatever.

Jake wants the money to send his mom to see *her* mom.

That is *painfully* kind.

I might vomit. Or try to kiss him. Hopefully not both at the same time.

"See any good spots?" Jake asks, oblivious to my emotional annihilation as we wander into the bedding section.

I suddenly feel very much like two teenagers in the bedding section of Macy's. An employee tracks us with suspicious eyes as we roam around the floor, searching for a good hiding place.

I clear my throat and shake away thoughts of vomiting and kissing. I need to focus on the task at hand. And then I see it. And I start giggling.

"What?" Jake asks, whipping his head around.

"Flannel." I point to a bed made up with a red-and-green checkered blanket.

We both look at Jake's shirt, and he laughs, eyes lighting up. "What can I say?" He shrugs. "I like what I like." He seems to hold my gaze a second longer than necessary when he says that. *And you know what, Jake Kaplan? I like what I like too.*

I glance behind us and am relieved to find that the employee tracking us is now busy helping a customer. At first I want to hide the voucher inside of a pillowcase, but we'd better not make this hunt too difficult or disruptive, so we just put it under the pillow instead. And then the next hour zips by as we traverse the rest of the mall, dodging hordes of shoppers as we hide a voucher for *Time Stands Still* in the jewelry and watch department and a voucher for *Animal Farm* in Pet Depot and a voucher for *Green Eggs and Ham* in Williams-Sonoma.

After hiding the final voucher, *Through the Looking Glass*

in Pearle Vision, we make our way back to Once Upon, and my heart starts pounding with adrenaline because oh my god, the event begins in ten minutes. We've passed out tons of flyers, baked a trough of cookies, gathered gift certificates for raffles, and Santa and our makeup artists are ready to go. But will it be enough to turn sales around? Enough to prove to Myra the store is worth keeping open? I tug on the chain of my necklace, fingers tracing the Star of David. I just don't know.

The mall music pauses after its eight hundredth play of "Rudolph," and someone makes an announcement about holiday hours.

Hmm.

An announcement.

I stop walking. Jake notices and raises an eyebrow. "What is it?"

I look up at the ceiling speakers and then back at him with a smile. "I have an idea."

"Of course you do, Shoshanna." He shakes his head, eyes lit with amusement. "Of course you do."

With so little time left until the event, Jake returns to the store to finish setup, and I spin right back around and walk through the mall in search of a directory marquee, which is something I've used exactly zero times since starting work here. I finally find a board and squeeze myself through the throng of people to read it. My pulse races as I scan the list of indexed stores. *Come on . . . Come on . . . There it is!* At the very bottom in tiny white script, right between Bath & Body Works and Claire's: *Security Office.*

There are only a few minutes left until the event begins, so I put my Olympic-level skills to the test. I spin, barrel, and duck my way through the mall to get to the security office in record time. Panting slightly, I knock on the door twice, and it opens a moment later. A woman in blue slacks and a white polo appraises me with a bored expression. "Someone shoplift?" she asks.

"Nope!"

"You have to call the police for physical fights, or—"

"Nothing like that," I cut her off, then smile and sweeten my voice. "May I, uh, come inside?" I scan her shirt for a name tag. "Ms. Hendricks."

She narrows her eyes but opens the door a little farther so I can step into the small room. There are dozens of monitors showing footage of the entire mall. It's surreal seeing it like this, a bird's-eye view of my habitat. We look like a bunch of ants, filing up and down hallways like we're all programmed on the same mission. But there's no time to critique the toxicity of mass consumption, especially when I need to wield that mass consumption in my favor.

"So. What is it?" Ms. Hendricks asks, settling into her chair.

"Well." I rock back on my heels and keep my voice sweet. Hopefully sweet. Hopefully not annoying. "I was wondering if I could make just a teeny-tiny announcement over the PA system to promote an event at Once Upon."

Okay, yes, I don't have the best history in the world with acceptable PA system announcements, but the lovely Ms. Hendricks doesn't need to know that. And *yet* it's almost like she can sniff out my PA system impulse-control issues. "Definitely not," she replies. And then she grabs her drink, a cup from Bo's Burritos. My eyes narrow in on the cup as she sips what is mostly melted ice.

"I could get you a refill," I offer. "I have an in at Bo's."

"Refills are free." But she appraises me carefully now. "Though, I wouldn't mind some chips and queso along with my refill of Coke."

"Done!" I squeal, a bit too loud for the tiny room.

Ms. Hendricks winces. "Fine." She leans forward and grabs a piece of paper. "But you're not making the announcement. I am. Write down what you want." She slides the paper and a pen my way.

I salute her. "Yes, ma'am."

She gives me a weird look and then shakes her head. "You know what? I'll take a side of guac as well."

I make it back to Once Upon just as Ms. Hendricks interrupts "Santa Baby" to deliver the announcement: "Attention, all holiday shoppers! The 'Grinch who Stole Bookmas' event has officially begun at Once Upon. Join the party for story time, snacks, face paint, and you might even meet Santa! Make this holiday season a happy one with your favorite local bookstore!"

"Who needs a walkie-talkie when you have the entire mall speaker system?" Myra asks. I turn to find her next to me, her BOOK BABE mug in hand. "Nice turnout," she comments, gesturing to the crowd.

"Thank you," I say, barely able to believe the amount of people in front of me.

As Myra goes to help someone in the romance section, I take in our absolutely jam-packed store. My pulse races as I observe everyone from random holiday shoppers to our most loyal customers. Ms. Serrano chats with some new faces by the nonfiction shelves while Mr. and Mrs. Murillo host story time in the children's section. Geraldine and Elliot will be by soon to face-paint, and Santa's big entrance is only minutes away. Kids and grown-ups alike are devouring Santa cookies and dreidel cookies and are ladling out cups of cider. A line for the registers snakes twenty customers long, giving even Make You Up a run for its money. Daniel checks out shoppers with the superhuman speed of a hero in one of his graphic novels.

I bounce on my heels. *Whoa*. This could actually freaking work.

We could actually save the store.

I breathe out deeply, and then a cute little kid is running up to me. "I found a voucher!" they proclaim, a *Where the Wild Things Are* voucher in hand.

"The first one!" I cheer. "Congratulations to you! Let's grab your book—oh, and these are your parents? Hello, welcome to Once Upon! Have you been here before?"

As the event goes on, my heart feels like it might burst with happiness, which would be really inconvenient, but *wow* this event is incredible. Geraldine and Elliot up their face-painting game to the next level. Santa shows up with— to my utter shock and complete delight—Cheyenne the Elf at his side. We have all four registers open, yet the line of customers never shortens, replenishing with new shoppers every time someone is checked out. At one point there's even a bout of impromptu karaoke led by Lola and Tanya, even though we don't have a karaoke machine. Or microphones. So they just kind of shout along to the music, and everyone sings "Jingle Bells" and then "(I've Had) The Time of My Life" from *Dirty Dancing*.

I'm about to join in when a familiar voice calls my name. "Shoshanna!"

And then another familiar voice. "Hey, darling!"

I spin around, and my mouth drops open as I see my moms threading their way between the aisles. Mama holds a bag of dreidels and chocolate coins, and Mom holds a platter of—

My eyes widen. "Did y'all bring latkes?"

Mom smiles. "We know they aren't as good cold, but we figured your holiday party could use a little more Hanukkah spirit."

"And that we could make up for missing Latkepalooza," Mama adds. "It was Mom's idea."

"*Y'all*," I say, not even embarrassed when my voice cracks on the word. "That's really nice. Thank you."

Mom puts down the tray of latkes and then steps forward and squeezes my hand, locking her eyes with mine. Her scent is comforting, familiar; it's the perfume she spritzed every day in her bedroom, while she put on makeup at her vanity and I rummaged through her cosmetic bags. I inhale it as she says, "Shoshanna, I know we already talked about it, but we wanted to make sure you know we're here for you. Always. Whether or not . . ." She clears her throat. "No matter what happens between your mama and I, we will always be a family. That is *never* going to change."

Mama steps forward too and takes my other hand. "We love you, sweet, brilliant, *sensitive* daughter. We love you more than anything. We're so proud to be your moms."

I take a steadying breath as I look at both of them, at the familiar faces that have been there for me throughout my entire life. Yes, I want my moms to stay together, and I'll be heartbroken if they separate, but—I realize I will be okay no matter what happens between them. I glance around the store, at our loyal customers, at my incredible friends, at this party I put together with the help of those who love me, and then back at my moms who raised me and will always support me, and I know I can handle anything.

"I love you guys too," I say, then jump forward and wrap my arms around both of them. The hug is tight and warm, and any bit of tension I was holding on to falls away in their embrace.

The party continues. My moms stay for latkes and cookies, and then they ask who else made the cookies, which leads to a very red-faced introduction between them and Jake—the only red face being mine, but trust me, it's red enough for all of us. When he returns to the registers, Mama gives me a *look*, and Mom literally freaking winks. My *Oh my god* groan can be heard all the way at the North Pole.

Eventually they leave to run a couple of errands and promise to be back to take me home after the party ends. And then there's more karaoke. And then all of the vouchers are found except for one. And, yes, Jake told me no one was going to find the *Rainbow Fish* voucher sealed in a baggie and weighted down with change at the bottom of the wishing fountain, and it seems he was correct. Most shoppers trickle out of the store, headed to their holiday celebrations. I thank Cheyenne and Geraldine profusely for all of their help before they hug me goodbye. Some of our regulars linger, and it turns into a more intimate party, the chatter cozy and familiar.

I finish helping a straggler customer in the young adult section just as Jake walks over to me, hesitant smile on his lips. My breath hitches as he scratches his neck. Dear lord. That neck. "Think we did it?" he asks. "Sold enough books to save the store?"

Tension straightens my spine. "I don't know. It seems like it." My eyes meet his, and a flash of excitement beats through me. "I hope so."

Before he can respond, the PA system clicks on, and Myra's voice plays overhead: "Everyone grab a drink and meet in the children's section for a toast!"

Jake and I walk to the scavenged refreshments table and a pour a glass of cider each. I glance at his lips as he drinks, then smile into my cup. "Shall we?" he asks.

My cheeks heat, and I nod. We walk to the back of the store as the rest of the employees gather. My pulse races when I look at Myra sitting before us all. Her husband stands next to her, and they're wearing matching ugly Christmas sweaters with horribly stitched reindeers on them. Myra looks out over all of us and smiles; glows, even. My heart thumps. It's a big smile. We must have sold enough books. Surely we did.

Myra clinks her glass, and all the chatter fades away as she addresses us. "It's certainly been an interesting holiday season. Thank you all for this wonderful party. I'm grateful to celebrate the holidays with my Once Upon family. You all hold a special place in my heart. Now, as many of you know, we've been running a little competition this week to see who can sell the most books, and I'm proud to announce our winner is none other than . . . Shoshanna Greenberg! Come on over here, Shoshanna!"

Myra beams at me, and for a half second I think, *Oh my god, I won!* But then I remember the reality, and I'm not going to take this money, not if it can help the store. There's scattered applause, and Jake nudges my shoulder and mouths, *Congrats. You earned it.*

"Thanks," I say. And I did earn it. But I don't want it. Still, it would be strange to turn down the money in front of everyone, so I walk toward Myra. She holds out a crisp check, and I accept it automatically and look down at the $250 amount, enough to fix Barbra like I set out to do in the first place.

"Great job," Myra tells me. I try to read into her expression, but she's giving nothing away. My fingers close around the check as she turns back to the crowd. "All right, everyone! Back to partying!"

Lola cranks up the music again, and the crowd disperses to eat up the remaining food and play some kind of nerd card game, but I stay standing in front of Myra, my heart pounding in my ears. "Can I talk to you for a minute?" I ask her. "Maybe in your office?"

"Sure," she responds easily, like she knew the question was coming. "I'll be right back, honey," she tells her husband.

"Oh, no problem," he says. "There's a peppermint-bark cookie left with my name on it." He leans down to kiss her on the lips and then walks off to the snack table.

Myra and I head to her office. Once inside, I pull the door closed behind us and hand the check back to her. "Here. Use it to keep the store open. Please."

"Shoshanna—" she says. And her expression shifts, barely, but it's enough to drop a pit in my stomach.

Oh.

Her eyes are soft. She squeezes her hands together, and when she speaks, I can hear the slightest wobble in her voice. "*Shoshanna*," she repeats.

I shake my head, moisture pricking my eyes. "You don't have to explain."

"Oh, I know I don't." She grins then, just a little, and it eases the hard knot in my throat the slightest bit. "But I want to. Come on. Sit down."

I sit in one of the chairs, and she moves in front of me, her eyes level with mine. "I love this store," she tells me. "It's like my child. I raised her from the ground up, poured all of my heart and time into her well-being, surrounded her with . . . let's call you aunts and uncles and cousins. This store, this wonderful store, has meant everything to me. I had a passion, and I pursued it tirelessly." She leans back, and a serene smile crosses her face. "But today you made me realize it's time to let go. You made me realize it's time to close Once Upon."

"What?" My pulse skips. "You mean it's my fault?"

"No, no," she quickly corrects. "I'm sorry, mamaleh. I didn't mean it like that. I meant—I meant today was incredible. The crowds, the love, the warmth. It was everything I love about this store tied up with a Christmas bow. But your passion to keep this store open made me realize I've lost mine. I still love Once Upon, but I'm focused on my writing now. I'm ready to turn the page."

"Nice pun," I say weakly.

"Thanks." She glances at her wall, covered in photos from past events, book signings and story hours. "It's been a fight to keep these doors open since day one. And although I appreciate the effort you put in—" She looks back at me. "I realized if I really wanted to keep this store open, then I would have found a way, like I always have. But no. I'm ready to move on. I see that now. I'll tell everyone after the holidays, and I'll make sure we're still open for a few months so they can find work elsewhere."

Myra's words wash over me and spread feelings of sadness and defeat. Of course she needs to do what's best for her. This is her life. And yet, the selfish thought crosses my mind: *What about me?*

What about *me* when Once Upon closes?

"Do you understand?" Myra asks.

I nod, throat tight. "Yes."

"The party was incredible," she repeats. "You're incredible. You're creative and caring, and you've got a lot of people who love you." She pauses, then says, "I love you, Shoshanna."

I glance down at my feet, then back up to Myra. Her smile is so genuine I can feel it course through me like the sweetest peppermint mocha in the world. "So." I grin at her. "Is it cool if I tell everyone I'm your favorite employee?"

"Well don't rub it in their faces," she teases.

I gasp. "Is that an admittance?"

"Oy vey."

Myra laughs, and I do as well, and the tension drains out of me. I love Myra, and I love this store, and I want it to stay open. But Myra is right, and my moms are right. I am smart and caring, and I have incredible people in my life. And as long as those things are true, I'll be okay. I'll be more than okay.

"Now take this," Myra says. She holds up the check and nudges it in my direction. "You earned it."

It's cold outside. Freezing, actually. My phone reads thirty-one degrees. People are still keeping the party going, and my moms won't pick me up for another fifteen minutes. But Once Upon is closing, and for the moment, I need a physical barrier to keep from sharing that news.

I stuff my hands into my pockets. My fingers brush against the check, folded once and shoved down deep for safekeeping. It'll be nice to get Barbra working again. But in a few months, I'm not sure where I'll be driving her.

"Shoshanna?" I spin around and find Jake behind me. He's wearing my purple scarf, and his skin is already flushed from the cold. I inhale as he steps forward, his concerned eyes trained on mine. "You ran out after talking to Myra. Did she—is the store closing?"

Silence beats heavy for a long moment. Finally, I manage a one-word reply. *"Yeah."*

And then my face crumples, and without thinking, I move toward him, and he moves toward me, and I hug him, and he hugs me back, and it's a serious full-body, two-armed hug, and he's warm, and he still smells like a freaking buttered croissant, and the tension eases from my muscles as I relax into his arms. I can feel his soft pulse in his throat and a little stubble from his jaw, and I think maybe if I could stay here forever, then I really wouldn't care about a bookstore closing.

Jake adjusts, just a slight shift but enough to snap me back to reality.

I slink out of his arms and rub my cold nose, the only part of me not suddenly heated. "Sorry," I say. "I know it's just a bookstore."

"Don't be sorry," Jake replies. "I know how much you love that place. And, whether you believe it or not, I like bookstores as well."

I laugh. "Even though you're not a reader?" I expect him

to smile back, but he hesitates, scratching his ear and glancing up at the sky. *Darn it. Seriously, what is wrong with me?* "I'm—"

Jake returns his gaze to mine. "The thing is," he says, "books are expensive. And you need a car to get to the library, or time to take the bus, which is hard when you're working a lot."

Oh. Of course.

"I'm a jerk," I tell him.

"You're really not." He runs a hand through his curls. "It's just stuff you haven't had to think about, you know?"

And I do know. I know exactly what that weird feeling is to watch someone hand over a credit card without a hint of concern when you're constantly tabulating every purchase. And yet I'm so lucky, so privileged, that books have never been a scarcity in my life.

"I'm sorry, Jake," I say. "Really."

His smile is soft. He glances back at the mall. "Do you want to come back inside?"

"No. Um, my moms will be here soon. Do you need a ride?"

Jake shakes his head. "My mom is coming in an hour."

"Okay. Well, tell her hi. And I'll see you tomorrow—" I break off because I won't see him tomorrow. Because tomorrow is Christmas, and the store will be closed until next year, and I don't know if he'll still be working here next year. And next year will only be a few months, anyway, and then we'll all be gone. And then I won't see Jake Kaplan anymore. And damn, that really sucks on top of all the suck.

Jake clears his throat, then looks down at the sidewalk, suddenly self-conscious in a way so cute I want to murder him. "Mom and I are having Chinese for lunch tomorrow. Want to join us? You could invite your moms, too."

"Yeah." I beam at him. "That would be nice. Text you later?"

Jake nods, and then he steps forward and very awkwardly kisses the top of my head, and then I hear him mutter, "*Wow, weird move, Kaplan*," as he walks back into the mall. I sit down on a bench and pat the top of my curls with a slight smile.

Weird move, indeed, Kaplan.

Geraldine: We can come over

Cheyenne: I have an entire box of peppermint chocolate truffles. Mom got them at work.

Geraldine: We can watch Time Stands Still. The second one that was so bad it's a comedic masterpiece.

Cheyenne: We can watch Time Stands Still AND eat this box of peppermint chocolate truffles

Shoshanna: I'm okay y'all

Shoshanna: Seriously. I promise. Enjoy your Christmas Eve.

Geraldine: But are you sure? Because we love you.

Cheyenne: We love you very much

Shoshanna: I'm sure

And I *am* okay. For the first time in a week, I feel like I can breathe. I've been wound so tight, trying so hard to fix everything, that it's actually a relief to finally accept I'm the only person I have control over. YouTubers decide when they're ready to post their content online. Married people decide whether or not they want to stay married. And bookstore owners decide if they no longer want to be bookstore owners.

My phone beeps again, and I go to check the group chain, but instead I find a text from Jake: Chinese food tomorrow?

I text back immediately because screw trying to be cool by waiting an appropriate amount of time to respond: Definitely. I got you a present, too.

Jake: Liar. What is it?

Shoshanna: Patience is a virtue.

Jake: Hmph. Your moms joining us?

I hesitate because I haven't worked up the nerve to ask them yet. After a moment, I say: Maybe. Will let you know in the morning. See you tomorrow!

Jake sends a smiley-face emoji.

I have a feeling Jake isn't one to send emojis lightly. I smile at the smiley-face emoji for a solid ten seconds. Adrenaline pulses through me, fast and frantic, and at first I'm not sure what to do with it, but then I realize suddenly, desperately,

I want to write. So I put away my phone, turn on my computer, scroll to the bottom of my document, and do just that.

The sun is barely a slip of orange on the horizon when Henry takes Isobel's hands in his own. Her eyes are soft, and her skin is callused from years of working in the armory. "I think I've always loved you," Henry says.

"Yeah?" Isobel steps forward and sighs. "About time you figured that out."

I write and write, and the sentences turn into paragraphs and the paragraphs into pages, and the entire book begins to open up in front of me, and I know where to take this story tomorrow and the days after that, and I can't wait to write those words. When I go to bed that night, I don't worry about my moms or Once Upon or anything else. Instead, I just fall asleep and dream about my characters.

Chapter Fifteen

Even though it's only eight in the morning, I'm already awake when I hear a knock on my door. I've been reading in bed for the last hour because, despite my best effort to sleep in, I'm now used to waking up at an ungodly hour for work.

I put my book down, then shift to sit up against my headboard and say, "Come in."

Mom opens the door and steps into my room. She's wearing leggings and an oversize sweater she probably found in the men's section of a thrift store. Her hair is up in its catastrophe bun. She looks beautiful. "Merry Christmas, sweet daughter," she says. "Should we go see what presents Santa left under the tree?"

"I think I'm on the naughty list." I sigh. "Something about not believing in our lord and savior Jesus Christ."

"Drat." Mom tsks, and we both laugh. "Hey, you want to go on a walk? With Mama, too. It's freezing, but we can bring hot chocolate."

"Sure," I say, tentative. "That sounds nice."

Ten minutes later, I have a puffy coat on over my pj's, and we're outside, hands curled around thermoses of hot chocolate. It feels like Christmas. And it's not just the yard decorations, though our neighbor's full set of electric reindeer, sled, and Santa certainly adds to the ambience. The world feels settled, everyone at home, gathered around with their families. I'm with my family. My moms and I walk down the streets we've walked down for years. Today is a little different. Their hands aren't clasped, and Mom falls in line with me more than Mama, but we're all here together. And that's something. It really is.

"We're sorry about Once Upon, darling," Mama says. She starts walking in the gutter, one foot directly in front of the other like a tightrope walker.

I told them last night about the store closing. Every time I say it out loud, it feels a little more real and less like some strange dream I can't shake off. "Thanks." I pull on one of my curls and loop it around my finger. "I'll find another job."

"We know you will." Mom knocks into my shoulder. "I'll never forget my first job. Ice cream scooper at Shelly's Iced Delights. Had a wrist injury by the end of summer and over-dosed on ice cream. Couldn't eat it again for years."

Mama laughs. "Sounds better than my first gig. Babysitter for *triplets*. They were four-year-old nightmares. I have never recovered."

"I guess I'm lucky," I say, blinking up into the sky. The morning sun pierces through soft white clouds. "Having a first job I love so much." *Loved*. We're in a cul-de-sac now. Through the windows, I can see one neighbor's Christmas tree glowing with strung lights. "Um." I turn to my moms, my cheeks already reddening at the question. "So, Jake invited me to Chinese lunch with his mom today. And invited y'all, too. Want to come?"

They exchange one of those parent-telepathy looks. My stomach tightens as they decide. I honestly don't know what outcome I want. If they say yes, embarrassment awaits. If they say no, it means they don't want to spend more time together. After a long beat, they look back at me.

"Love Chinese food," Mama says.

"As long as there's General Tso's on the table, I'm in," Mom tells me.

I grin. "I think that can be arranged."

We start moving again, Mama tight-roping along the cul-de-sac's curved gutter. We walk for a full hour and talk about everything, all of the shenanigans at the mall, Cheyenne's rekindled relationship and Geraldine's YouTube career, how Mom is going to search for a new job herself next year, because she deserves to be paid more for the hours she puts in, and how Mama feels so fulfilled volunteering for art classes at the senior center. There's a sharp chill in the air, but each sip of hot chocolate creates a burst of warmth.

* * *

Chu's Kitchen is packed. Boisterous families cram into every available seat and pass dishes and menus around. There are a lot of curls and kippahs and so much laughter, and I love it all. A busboy wipes down our table as a waitress seats us. We all slide into the large booth, Jake and Ms. Kaplan on one side and my moms and me on the other. Jake and I both sit on the inside, and I swear he nudges my shoe with his own on purpose. I smile as I grab a crispy noodle and dip it into the dish of duck sauce.

"Thank you for inviting us," Mama says, pushing up the sleeves of her purple sweater. The restaurant is warm and filled with the heavenly smells of garlic and onion.

"Of course! We're so glad you could join us!" Ms. Kaplan replies. "Oh, I just love Christmas! It's my favorite holiday. Everyone is off work. I get to spend all day with my sweet Jakey. I love any excuse to eat Chinese food. *And* I don't have to go to synagogue. Perfect holiday, right?"

Mom laughs. "Pretty perfect."

"Also, I love eggnog," Ms. Kaplan adds.

I nod. "Eggnog is delicious."

"Do you guys trust me?" Jake asks as a waiter passes us menus.

I tilt my head. "Do we trust you?"

"He wants to show off and order for the table," Ms. Kaplan explains. "It's male chauvinism, and I wouldn't stand

248

for it, but the boy has good taste buds. Chu's might run a Jake Kaplan special menu next year."

Jake laughs and rubs the back of his head. "But seriously, no pressure if you want to order your own food."

"I'm in," Mama says, flinging her menu down on the table.

"As long as there's General Tso's," Mom adds.

"But of course," Jake replies. "They have the best in the city."

"Perfect." Mom smiles and grabs the teapot to fill up her cup. Ms. Kaplan holds up her cup to be filled as well, while Mama compliments her on her bracelet. We're all so comfortable already. It feels natural, easy. But that can happen when you're surrounded by members of the tribe.

"What about you?" Jake asks. His eyes meet mine as our moms chat. "Do you trust me?"

My cheeks heat as I nibble on another crispy noodle. "I sure as heck didn't a week ago," I reply.

"One week." Jake shakes his head. "Is that really when we met?"

"Unbelievable, right?" I ask.

It *is* unbelievable. Because looking at this guy across the table from me, this guy with a crooked left eyebrow and magical baking powers, this guy who deserves a better dad but seems to be the best son a mom can ask for, this guy who can rock the heck out of a flannel, it feels like this guy has been in my life a lot longer than one week.

"So what about now?" he asks. "Trust me now?"

"Now . . ." I grab another crunchy noodle, and Jake does as well. His eyes flash when our hands brush together, and a jolt of electricity runs up my spine. "Now . . . maybe my feelings have changed."

We spend a full two hours at the restaurant. Every time one of us stops eating, another begins again, and then by the time they stop, someone else realizes they can eat a little more, and so on. By the end of it all, we've devoured the platters of General's Tso's, orange beef, Chinese broccoli, and chow mein, and there's only an errant noodle or orange slice left.

I lean back against the booth and groan. "I don't think I'll ever be able to eat again."

"Don't say that," Jake replies quickly.

"Why?"

He hesitates. "Because . . . reasons . . ."

I'm about to interrogate him more when the check arrives at the table, and our moms do the squabble over wanting to pay. *I invited you all! But we had more people eating!* Jake and I offer to help pay as well, but we're both shushed with ferocity so intense that we break into stomach-holding laughter. Eventually they come to a compromise, and minutes later, we're heading out into the parking lot. The wind has kicked up since this morning, so blustery it'll probably take two rounds of conditioner and the big paddle brush to detangle my curls tonight.

We all walk toward our cars. Our moms chat at full

speed, but Jake clears his throat to interrupt them. "Um, hey. So . . ." Everyone turns to him, and I can't stop grinning at his discomfort. "I was hoping to take Shoshanna somewhere . . . I mean, if you want to go?" He looks at me, and I have no idea what he has planned, but of course I nod *yes*. "Great!" He flashes a smile so genuine I could die on the spot. "So Mom, can I use the car, and maybe Shoshanna's moms can take you home? If that's okay with everyone?"

All three moms are grinning at him like absolute fools, and I snicker as Jake lifts his arms and then forces them back down, like he's resisting the urge to shove his face in his hands. "You two are very cute," Ms. Kaplan says.

"*So* cute," Mama agrees.

"Y'all, please stop," I say, cheeks burning but at least not as badly as Jake's.

"Stop what?" Mom asks. "Talking about how very cute you two are?"

"Do you have the keys?" I ask Jake. "Because if not, I'm sure I can YouTube how to hot-wire a car."

My pulse skips when he laughs. "Yes, I have the keys. Let's get out of here."

"Have fun, you two!" Ms. Kaplan calls after us.

"Be home by six!" Mama shouts.

It's possible Mom adds something about kissing, but thankfully by then I've had the good sense to stuff my fingers in my ears.

* * *

Gary's diner is a double-wide trailer that's been turned into a restaurant. It sits alone in a gravel parking lot with a battered enamel sign that reads GARY'S in navy font with a chipped "A." Christmas lights dangle around the perimeter of the building, blinking in the overcast afternoon light. As we approach, I read a laminated sign on the door that says CLOSED FOR CHRISTMAS.

"I think it's closed for Christmas," I tell Jake.

He raises an eyebrow. "Good thing I have a key." He digs the key out of his pocket, unlocks the front door, and flicks on the lights. The inside is much cuter than the outside, retro with vinyl red booths, tabletops painted in different colors, and a front counter with swivel bar seats. A jukebox sits against a back wall, and after Jake plugs it in, the Temptations begin to play.

"Your mom would be so proud." I sit on one of the swivel seats as Jake walks around to the other side of the counter. "So . . . what are we doing here?"

But Jake doesn't answer my question.

Instead, Jake unbuttons his flannel shirt.

I start coughing and consider making a run for it or maybe taking my top off as well until I realize Jake is wearing a T-shirt underneath the flannel. *Right. Keep your clothing on, Shoshanna. First-date rule number one, if this is a date, which it's probably not, but maybe it is, and oh my god, am I on a date with Jake Kaplan right now?*

I clear my throat as he grabs an apron and throws it on over his T-shirt.

"We are here," Jake finally answers, now walking back to the open kitchen and pulling out a couple of stainless-steel bowls. "To make dessert!" He grins at me from behind the counter. "And you're helping."

"Am I?" I ask, but I'm already sliding off the stool to join him in the kitchen. Playing hard-to-get is not my strong suit. "Oh, wait! Your present!"

I turn back around and dig through my tote bag. "Let me guess. . . ," Jake says. "Is it a book?"

"That would have been on brand, but you're incorrect." I find the present and then walk up to him and hand over the envelope. I rock back on my heels as he opens it. "I know it won't cover the full cost, but—" Jake's mouth parts as he pulls out the printed airline gift certificate. "It should cover part of the flight. I can fix Barbra whenever. It's not like she's going anywhere. Also, I don't know your mom's favorite airline, so hopefully—"

"Shoshanna," Jake cuts me off. I stop rambling and look up at him. When his dark eyes lock onto mine, I can feel my heart in my throat. *"Thank you."*

"Sure." I tug on my necklace. "Anyone would have done it."

"No." He shakes his head. "They really wouldn't have."

He keeps looking at me, like he might say something else, or *do* something else, but eventually he clears his throat and puts the envelope away in his back pocket. "Come on," he says. "Brownie time."

We get to baking, and I discover baking alone with Jake Kaplan is infinitely better than baking with Jake Kaplan and his mom and assorted friends because when I bake alone with Jake Kaplan, every now and then he'll nudge my shoulder, and every now and then I'll throw a pinch of flour at him, and every now and then he'll throw a glob of batter at me, and by the time the peanut butter truffle brownies are in the oven and we're both sitting on the stools out front, laughing and covered in various baking ingredients, he might say, "I really like you, Shoshanna Greenberg."

And I might say, "I really like you, Jake Kaplan."

And we might stare at each other with wide eyes for a really long time that would probably make our moms ask about a wedding date if they were here. Which, thank hashem, they're not.

When the brownies are done, Jake takes them out of the oven and serves them in bowls with two scoops of homemade vanilla ice cream. It smells like happiness, and I'm sure it'll taste like euphoria, but just as I lift up my spoon, Jake interrupts with an "Ooh!"

"What?" I ask, my eyes on the brownie.

"Look outside," Jake says. "It's snowing! On Christmas!"

I drag my gaze away from the brownie to look at him. "I didn't know you were so invested in Christmas, Mr. *Kaplan*."

"Ha, ha." He grins. "I'm not invested. But snow on Christmas in Georgia feels special. Even for us Jews. Don't you think?"

I glance out the window. Flurries fall and dance around the stringed lights. It is beautiful— magical, even. "Yeah," I agree, turning back to Jake. "Pretty darn special."

He laughs, and when his eyes flick back to mine, my stomach flips.

And when he takes my hand, my breathing hitches.

And when he says, "*Shoshanna*," I do a full-fledged swoon.

And when we lean forward to kiss, his lips warm against my own, I feel pleasure radiate through me from inside to out.

And when he pulls away with a soft smile, both of our cheeks flushed, he nods and says, "Pretty darn special, indeed."

Epilogue

B lack beans or pinto?" I ask.

"Pinto. Actually, let's do black beans." I begin to scoop when the guy says, "Actually, let's do half and half. That's not extra, is it? Is the guac extra?"

I keep a smile plastered onto my face as I slap his half-and-half beans into the bowl. "Not extra for the beans, but yes, guac is extra."

He rolls his eyes. "Of course it is."

I (barely) bite back the urge to say *I don't make the prices*, as he moves on to the next station and I move on to the next customer. It's April, and Once Upon closed its doors two weeks ago. Although it's hard to still work at the same mall, I wasn't going to pass up the job when Geraldine told me Bo's Burritos was hiring.

After another thirty minutes of slapping rice and beans into bowls, I finish my shift, hang up my apron, and walk over to the wishing fountain, where Geraldine and Cheyenne are hanging out before their shifts start.

"Friends!" I say.

"Friend!" they respond.

"Look at this." Geraldine shoves her phone in my face. "Three thousand views. Three thousand people watched my video, and not one of them hates me!"

"You're a rock star!" I say.

"Huh?" Cheyenne asks, looking up from her phone.

Geraldine rolls her eyes. "Seriously, Chey. You work in the same *mall* as your girlfriend, and you're still texting with her twenty-four-seven?"

"She doesn't work Sundays," Cheyenne points out while finishing her text. "I miss her."

"You literally saw her last night," Geraldine replies.

I snort, and then my own phone buzzes. I pull it out to find a message from Mom, a thumbs-up and a fingers-crossed emoji. She had a job interview today, and according to the emojis, it sounds like it went well! My moms have been in therapy for a few months now, but it's still too soon to say what will happen with them.

"Is that Jake?" Cheyenne asks, passing me her milkshake.

"Chocolate strawberry?" I check.

She nods. "But of course. I'm not a chocolate-banana monster like Geraldine."

"Hey!" Geraldine shouts, sipping on her own milkshake.

I laugh. "And no, not Jake. My mom— Wait." My phone buzzes again with another text, and this one is from Jake.

Jake: If you pick me up from work later, I'll bake you mint fudge brownies.

Me: 100% deal. Barbra Streisand and I will be there at 8.

My cheeks warm as I put my phone back down. Cheyenne and Geraldine exchange a look.

"They're so cute," Cheyenne says.

"Painfully cute," Geraldine agrees.

Then Cheyenne's eyes lock on something in the distance. "Hey, is that Daniel?"

My pulse picks up as I scan the Sunday mall crowd, and sure enough, I find Daniel and Lola standing in line for smoothies. I can even see Daniel's Spider-Man socks from here! It was hard when Myra told everyone the news, and even harder when I told Daniel I'd known that news for a couple of weeks. He wasn't mad at me or anything like that, but it still pushed some sort of invisible distance between us—or maybe that was the physical distance. I haven't seen him since he got a job at his university bookstore in February. Though he did snap me a picture of their newly improved shelves thanks to his recommendations, and I did send him a link to my review of that *Sleepwalker* graphic novel—it was as awesome as he promised.

"Be right back!" I shout at my friends, and then race up to Daniel and Lola.

She spies me first, eyes brightening, her hair now blue instead of pink. "Shoshanna!"

"Hey!" Daniel says.

"What are y'all doing here?" I ask. "How are classes? I miss you!"

We chitchat for a few minutes when Lola suddenly lowers her voice to a conspiratorial whisper. "You heard the news, right?"

"*Lola.*" Daniel nudges her arm.

I narrow my eyes. "What news? Is this a Marvel thing?"

"Tell her!" Lola insists.

Daniel sighs and rubs a hand over his hair. "I was going to wait until I knew for sure. I don't want to get your hopes up."

"Well, now you *have* to tell me."

"Okay." Daniel takes a breath and then looks both ways. "All right."

"*Daniel,*" I say.

"Okay!" He claps his hands together and locks eyes with me. "I heard that Myra was talking with Ms. Serrano. And Ms. Serrano said she couldn't imagine her life without Once Upon in it, and she was bored with the whole retirement thing anyway, so—"

"Shut up!" I scream the words so loud that half the people in the food court start to stare at me, but I could not care less. Adrenaline pulses through my veins as I turn to Lola. "Is he saying what I think he's saying?" I turn back to Daniel. "Are you saying what I think you're saying?"

"Oh!" He holds a hand to his chest. "Am I allowed to talk now?"

"Shut up, yes," I tell him.

He grins. "Yes. I'm saying what you think I'm saying. Ms. Serrano is buying the store. Papers are getting signed next week. Once Upon is—"

"—starting its next chapter!" I shout.

"Nice pun," Lola says.

"Impressive," Daniel agrees.

I'm smiling so hard, I can feel it down to my toes. "I know, right?"

Acknowledgments

Mom and Dad, you are both texting me as I write these acknowledgments. I couldn't be more grateful to have such a close relationship with my parents. I love you both an infinite amount. Thank you for always fostering my love of reading and writing and for being there for me on every occasion.

Elise LaPlante, you are my person. I can't wait to watch you cry again when you read these acknowledgments. I love you a gross amount and am obscenely lucky to call you my best friend.

Bubbie and Papa Bobby, I'm grateful to have two incredible grandparents in my life. I love you both and look forward to many more phone chats and visits. Lauren Sandler Rose and Melissa Sandler, thank you for being exceptionally amazing cousins. I love you both and am grateful that, despite living so far apart from each other, we are only growing closer each year.

Kiki Chatzopoulou, Anna Meriano, and Amanda Saulsberry, although we no longer live in the same place, we still talk most days, and that brings me so much comfort and happiness. Thank you for always being there to confide in and to bring a smile to my face. Love y'all!

Rachael Allen, Lauren Vassallo, and Kayla Whaley, thank you for reading this book in various pieces and stages and helping me work through it. I wouldn't be able to write without critique partners, and I'm grateful to have such excellent ones in my life.

Jim McCarthy, this past week marked our five-year anniversary. Each year I'm happier than the last to have you as my agent. Thank you for all your guidance and support and for answering the approximately three million emails I've sent you.

McElderry Books, thank you for welcoming me to your imprint. Kate Prosswimmer, it's been such a joy working with you, and I hope to do so again many times in the future. Thank you for your wonderful notes and warm encouragement. Thank you also to Nicole Fiorica, Justin Chanda, Shivani Annirood, Chantal Gersch, and the rest of the team for all your hard work and support. And thank you to Maggie Cole, the brilliant artist behind this cover.

Thank you also to all these wonderful people for their support: Rebecca Arnall, Kelly Bryan, Kayla Burson, Alison Doherty, Brittany Kane, Deborah Kim, Katie King, Katie

Locke, Katherine Menezes, Christy Michell, Harmony Viray, and Randy Winston.

As always, I'm already worried and embarrassed I'm missing people, so to those people, I apologize for having a terrible memory, and *thank you, thank you, thank you.*

I took *write what you love* to heart with this book, so thank you to my list of inspirations: *The Office, 10 Things I Hate About You, Emma, Clueless, You've Got Mail, Superstore, New Girl,* and *Crazy Ex-Girlfriend.*

And last but certainly not least, thank you to every incredible bookstore and bookseller out there. Thank you for making my life fuller, happier, and more inspired!

Love,

Laura